SHIPWRECKED WITH A SUITOR

EMILY MURDOCH

To Tom and Lily. Some of our dearest friends.
And of course, Joshua.

ACKNOWLEDGMENTS

This was the series that I never thought I could publish, so first thanks must go to my amazing Kickstarter supporters! Thank you for your faith in me, and I hope you love this book as much as I do!

Thank you to my wonderful editor, Julia Underwood, who has given me unparalleled advice – any mistakes left are completely my own!

Thank you to my glorious cover designer, Samantha Holt, a true artist whose patience with me is much appreciated.

Thank you to my ingenious formatter, Falcon Storm, whose willingness to format whenever I drop an unexpected email is fantastic!

And to my family. Thank you.

Merde! Now his shoes were wet, and the storm seemed to show no signs of abating.

Pierre d'Épiluçon glanced down at the bottom of the little boat that he had...requisitioned, and cursed again under his breath. This night had come down so fast, he could not even see the wooden slats that made up the bow of the boat.

But he could feel. His thin leather shoes, never intended for such an adventure as this, were soaked through.

Somewhere on this godforsaken boat, there was a leak.

With heavy head and numb fingers, Pierre forced his way against the wind to the other side of the small boat, and tried to pull a rope towards him. It was caught in the fierce gale that had overwhelmed him, not – what, twenty minutes before?

Twenty minutes that had felt like a lifetime.

This was ridiculous, what had he thought he was doing? His desperation to reach the shores of England, in any way possible, had now forced him in the middle of the Channel with no one to guide him, no map to aid him, no compass to solace him, and now this storm had turned him around so often that he had no idea which way France nor England truly lay. Those summers boating on the lake were nothing on this.

Pierre tasted bile in his mouth once more, and hurtled towards the edge of the boat, little as it was, to stick his head over. The knife wound in his thigh screamed out in pain.

After being violently sick, he slumped back and felt the freezing water reach his knees.

"*Ce n'est pas ce que j'avais imaginé*," he murmured to himself. "This is not what I had thought would happen."

But the words were lost to the wind, snatched out of his mouth by the storm that had robbed him of will, wind in his sails, and awareness of where he was.

If he did not find a shore soon, and he was beginning to wonder whether France really would be the worst thing in the world right now, then...well, there was glory in drowning, was there not?

Pierre closed his eyes, exhaustion overwhelming him for a moment. In his mind's eye, he saw what he had left behind in France.

His eyes snapped open. Anything but that.

Reaching down his hands to the wound, he tried to feel whether it had torn any further. No, it was still a few inches across, still bleeding heavily. It was tempting to give in to the desire to vomit again, but he must be strong. Surely, he would find the welcoming shores of England soon, even if it meant becoming a servant in that land.

Filled with renewed courage, but weakening with every moment as icy cold spray burst over the sides of the boat, Pierre rose and tried to concentrate, ignoring the pain in his thigh, the emptiness of his stomach, and the reeling of his head.

The stars ... he could navigate from the stars.

One throw of his head backwards told him that the gods were laughing at him that night. Of course he could not see the stars, there was a *stupide* storm!

He shivered, and tried to keep his balance as the little boat rocked against a huge wave. What had he been thinking? Why had he come straight from the town to the harbour, without provisions, without even changing out of his court clothes! Here he was, like the *imbécile* that he was, all lace and gold brocade, when what he really wanted right now was a greatcoat!

There! Was that a light? Pierre squinted, brushing salt-water out of his burning eyes, as he blinked desperately in the direction of what could be...could he have been dreaming?

No! There in the distance, perhaps four or five miles away – miles that felt insurmountable at present – was a light. It was flickering, it was small, it could not possibly be anything as substantial as a lighthouse, but it was surely real.

At least, it looked real. Whether it be shore or ship, it was people, and that was enough for freezing, injured Pierre.

The sail was of no use: torn to tatters by the blasted storm, there was nothing for it but to row. Pierre pulled at the oars and almost staggered back, astonished at their weight. That was the trouble with nobility, he smiled ruefully. They have not done a day's labour in their life.

Well, he was about to pay for all of that now. Ensuring that his back was to the light that seemed to glimmer and blind in the darkness, Pierre heaved, putting all his strength into the oars.

But there was not much left of his strength. Though he

pulled with all his might, there did not seem to be enough energy within him to survive.

Tirer, you fool, pull, Pierre told himself. Or make yourself a nice home here in the deep, for his backside and occasionally knees were covered in water.

More sinking than sailing, the boat moved slowly through the water. Every minute or so, Pierre had to pause the halting rhythm that he created, and check to see whether he was still going in the correct direction. His shoulders burned, and the place where he had been stabbed in the thigh seemed actually to be on fire, the salt scalding it with every moment.

Five minutes must have passed. Maybe ten. Now twenty? It was impossible for Pierre to tell, his golden pocket watch now full of seawater and for one moment, a scattering of seaweed. He cried out with the effort as he pulled the oars back another time, and yet he could not hear it. Shouting into that storm was akin to shouting into an abyss.

A heavy judder stopped the boat, and tipped it slightly on its side. Pierre, unprepared for such a movement, found himself vomiting slightly as he dropped an oar inside the boat.

"Now what?" He murmured, almost delirious with exhaustion. "Are we back in France again?"

But the boat was not moving. He could feel that now, feel the slow steady flow of the water that had crept into the boat start to settle. One exploratory hand wandered over the side of the boat, and the ocean felt sand, and rocks.

Pierre's brows furrowed. "The light."

He had recalled the reason for his desperate row. Turning around, he saw it: a flickering candle in the window of a house, a little worn down at the edges, just twenty yards from the beach where he had landed.

Pierre blinked. *The beach where he had landed.*

A shaking leg rose, and tipped him out of the boat. Pierre fell onto sand and rocks, and though they abraded his hands, they were more than welcome.

"Land," he muttered. "Even a shipwrecked man can find land."

Everything hurt, but there was no relief in his lungs, just air. He had managed it: he had not drowned, he had not let the storm take him!

Pierre almost laughed, but the sharp pain in his side prevented him, and the thought that he may be back in France sealed his mood. The rushing gale that had stormed his vessel on the open sea was still here, freezing his wet clothes to his skin.

France, or England? How to tell? There was no one here, it was the dead of night. If this was truly France, he needed to hide himself, to disappear in the night, so that no one could find him. If this was England, why, he had to find Paendly.

There was no time to lose. He had to move.

Pierre stood up, and the stars that had been missing from the night sky when he had desperately needed them to navigate, suddenly appeared. There was lightness in his head, and suddenly nothing hurt any more.

He collapsed in a dead faint.

A minute later, an hour, a day – who could tell? – Pierre groaned, and opened his eyes. It was still night – or it was night again. How long had he been unconscious?

The storm around him seemed to suggest that he had been out only a few minutes. Pierre lay, sprawled on the beach, the very image of a shipwrecked fool. The pebbles beneath him were scattered with rocks and a little sand, but it was a relief to have anything beneath him that wasn't swaying.

"*Mon Dieu*, what is to become of me?"

"What is your name?" cried the woman who suddenly appeared above him, glittering earrings almost blinding him as the light of her lamp shone through them.

～

"Ten minutes is all I need, and that is all I will take!"

"But Father – "

The door slammed, and Helena was left talking to an empty room.

She sighed, allowing all of the frustration in her lungs to leave her body. Well, there was nothing for it now. He had gone, as she knew he would, and in a few days when he came back, she would still be here waiting.

Helena rose with the two plates in her hand, and took them through to the back door, where they could be left to be rinsed by this terrible storm that had descended a few hours ago as the sun had gone down. It was impossible to prevent her father from visiting the Anchor Inn, and whenever he did – for those 'ten minutes' that he always promised her – he was always roped into some scheme or other with the other men of the village.

Last month they had gone to London, to seek their fortunes in the dock yards. The time before that – just before Easter, it had been – they had disappeared for a week when they had walked to Marshurst to see if there was any fieldwork.

Helena frowned as she looked at the mess he had left behind, and sighed, picking up a cloth and holding it outside a window for a few moments to get it nice and damp. Well, she and Teresa had made a choice: they would care for their father in the best ways that they knew. Teresa had gone to London to earn money, and Helena had stayed here to keep house for him.

The sadness that threatened her at every turn started to well up again, but she forced it down. She would see her sister again – sooner rather than later, she hoped. It had been too long: for too long had her poor sister been forced to –

She stopped in the middle of her thought as the sound of her stomach growling broke through even the noise of the gale. She smiled. Of course: when was the last time she had eaten? That morning? Perhaps last night?

Helena sighed, and looked around the house. It was a small one, smaller than even she had imagined when her father had told her that he had found the perfect place for them to live after their...reduction in circumstances. Four rooms, two downstairs and two upstairs. A kitchen of sorts, and a parlour, and two bedrooms upstairs. Nothing more, nothing less, and the fishing rights that had come with it – well, her father had dreamed.

She did not need to step through the parlour, where she was now wiping down the small table in the centre of the room, and into the kitchen, to know that there was little food in the house. The end of a loaf, some butter graciously given by the local milkmaid.

There was nothing for it; she would have to go outside, and check the crab nets.

Pulling on her father's greatcoat, and his wax hat that kept his balding head dry, Helena threw a quick glance at herself in the five-inch looking glass square that she kept in the window, by their candle. She loved the way that it doubled the light, and on the rare occasion that she wished to see her reflection...

Blonde straggling hair, unkept and unbrushed. Dark lashes circling startling blue eyes, eyes so light blue that they even caught her notice sometimes. A pair of rich pink lips, and a nose that she always said was too small for her face, but her father loved because it was her mother's.

Of course, at this moment she could barely see any of that, as her father's wax hat hid most of her. All to the better: anything to keep the storm from chilling her bones.

As soon as she stepped through the door, Helena started to regret her choice. Perhaps she should have checked, she thought as the gale howled against her, making every step feel almost impossible to make. There could have been an end of a loaf, perhaps some kippers from an earlier catch.

Her feet stumbled on the slippery rocks as she made her way doggedly to the crab traps. There were only six, and the first two were empty, her freezing fingers fumbling at the catchments. The third was full: four crabs, three of them small but one large. Helena smiled into the darkness of the night, and picked it up. It was easier to take the whole thing back with her.

Turning back towards home, something caught her eye to her right. She could not have said what it was; the flutter of that ragged white sail, perhaps, or the outline of a small boat on its side.

Whatever had first caught her attention, it was nothing to the figure on the ground that was moaning quietly.

Helena jolted, and dropped the crab cage. It cracked, leaving a hole through which the three small crabs escaped.

She barely noticed. Her eyes were affixed on the collapsed man in what looked like – a golden jacket?

This was not uncommon, of course. You did not live four

years in a fishing village without seeing the bodies of the drowned. But this was no working man; this was not a man accustomed to fish in the dead of night for crabs, or from dawn to dusk to find enough sustenance to fill your belly and your market stall.

Helena edged closer, her heart racing. He was wealthy, there was no doubt about that. His shoes were the flimsiest she had ever seen, and that meant money. Now that she was a little closer, she could see that the jacket was not made of gold, but embroidered so finely with gold thread that it seemed to shimmer and glitter with every movement that she made.

His hands were outstretched, as though he had been reaching for something. Helena stared at him, and then the direction which he was facing.

Her candle. The candle in the window: 'twas the only sign of civilisation for a mile in any direction. Her father had loved being far out from the town, and Helena had accepted it.

Now it may have saved this man's life.

Helena took another step towards him, and she swallowed down the nerves that she felt in being so close to a stranger. Why, he could be a vagabond, or a criminal! He could be anything or anyone, and here she was, alone with him in the dark!

The storm still pounded her with its gusts, and a drizzle of rain started to fall. She shivered, and took that final step to find herself beside the shipwrecked man.

For there was no doubt about that: his boat was done for, almost destroyed. But how far had he come, and why did he not dress more suitably?

"*Merci,* that will do nicely, *Jean-Paul,*" murmured the

man suddenly. "But the chicken will do for tomorrow, tell chef for me..."

Helena had jumped back, clutching her greatcoat around her against the battling wind, but the man did not seem to waken.

That had been French. He was a Frenchman! The nerves that had started to creep up her spine heightened at the knowledge. Why, were they not at war with France? Or Napoleon, at least; so out of the way as she was, she depended on Teresa's news to keep her abreast of foreign policy.

Well, if they were at war, then he was a prisoner of war, Helena reasoned with herself, teeth beginning to chatter. And a prisoner of war had no business being so wealthy.

She hated herself for it, but necessity drew it from her. Kneeling down hastily, she started to pat him down, looking for a pocket, a ring, a watch, anything of value.

A huge intake of breath and the opening of his eyes startled her as he rolled over onto his back, causing Helena to almost fall backwards onto the beach.

As she rose and peered over him, he shouted, making her jump again: "*Mon Dieu*, what is to become of me?"

Helena swallowed, and cried out against the gale: "What is your name?"

"Mademoiselle!" His eyes grew wide, wider than she thought possible, and in them she saw fear and confusion. "*Aidez-moi, s'il vous plaît*, I am lost, I am trying to find – "

He broke off: Helena, staring wildly into his dark brown eyes, taking in the sand splattered face, the paleness of his cheeks, and now the way that his hands were clutching at what appeared to be a bloody wound in his thigh.

"You – you are injured, sir!" She shouted, feeling stupid for stating the obvious but unsure exactly what else to say.

The man stopped moving, and stared at her in wonderment. "English?" He whispered.

Helena nodded, eyes transfixed on her Frenchman. It was not crab that the sea had delivered to her then, but sailor.

"English," he repeated under his voice, and then stronger, "*Pardon mademoiselle,* my English is not strong, but it should be enough. Please help me – take me inside, and warm me! I have friends, I have money, *s'il vous plaît...*"

Helena stared at him, and bit her lip. With her father gone to the Anchor – and then to goodness knows where – she would be alone in the house. Well, alone with him. Even soaked to the skin, exhausted, and what looked like stabbed, this Frenchman was still devilishly handsome. To be alone with him for a few hours would be...uncomfortable.

And what if anyone found out? An unmarried woman alone in a house with a man – and a Frenchman!

"*S'il vous plaît,*" he said faintly, and she saw the pallor on his face grow. "*Mademoiselle belle,* s'il vous plaît..."

It was not really a decision, after all. How could she leave this poor man, for all he was a Frenchman, to freeze, or drown, or die of his injuries?

"Try to stand up," she said moving quickly, pulling under his arms and struggling with all her might to raise him up. "'Tis not far."

---

2

*H*elena gasped at the weight of him, and tried to concentrate on exactly where she was placing her feet on the slippery rocks. The rain that was now sheeting down did nothing to aid her, and neither did the constant muttering and jerking of the man each time he stepped with his injured leg.

"*J'ai mal,*" he garbled in that strange tongue Helena was almost sure was French as she clutched at his gold brocade sleeve to steady him. "Ah, mademoiselle, if you only knew..."

"Tell me all about it later," Helena panted, affixing her eyes on the candle and finding to her dismay that, thanks to the pouring rain, she had been veering a little too much to the left.

A foot stumbled, and for a moment she was unsure whether it was her own or one of his; it did not matter really, for they both came tumbling down onto the slick wet rocks, and Helena felt the dull pain in her knees through her gown.

"Ah, *mes excuses*, I did not mean to – "

"Yes, well," Helena interrupted, now starting to regret her initial kindness that had so far led only to discomfort and actual bodily pain. "Least said, soonest mended. Here, let me help – "

The last word caught in her throat. Now that they were closer to her home, the little candlelight that her meagre candle created pooled across the man's face: and for the first time, she could see him clearly. What a specimen: what a man was this! Handsome, more handsome than any man that she had ever before beheld.

Short cropped hair, dark but that could have been the rain confusing the tint. Dark eyes, darker and richer brown than she had seen in this land. He was tall, undoubtedly, if he had not been crouching over his injured leg, and there was a haughtiness to his face that was not unbecoming. It said, I know my worth. It said, you are fortunate to see me. It said, I am nobility.

"Mademoiselle?" His voice broke through her thoughts, and she blinked at him. "Mademoiselle, are you well?"

Helena flushed in the freezing rain. "Quite well, thank you sir. We just need to get you out of this rain."

She had not thought to ask his name, and it was getting more difficult to hear each other as the storm railed down and brought heavier and heavier rain. Instead of more conversation, she thought, we need more movement.

Leaning down to heave him up once more, Helena was suddenly very conscious of just how close she was to this handsome man – closer than she had been to any man, come to think of it, fair or foul.

Her cheeks burned as she felt the taut strength of him, even though it was at this moment weak and uncontrolled. His feet slipped across the rocks as she bore him purposefully towards her door. It was so close now, and all she had to do was concentrate on that, and not the arm that was around her neck, and the hand whose fingers were now reclined in hers...

Her other hand reached out, and touched the safety of the sodden wood door. She had done it. They had made it, and not a moment too soon, for the gentleman – for gentleman he undoubtedly was – looked ready to pass out and collapse on her floor.

"Here we are," she said, thrusting him through the doorway. "Now, there is no bed for you I am afraid, sir, but we can – sir!"

She had let go of him for a split second to turn and shut the front door, and it had been a struggle as the gale had got up, and was fighting against her. In that short time, the man had keeled right over, and crashed his shoulder into the table as he sank to the floor.

"Giselle," he murmured, "is that you?"

Helena's face flushed at the sound of the woman's name. Who did she think she was – his lover?

But as she leant over him, a new focus for her attentions caught her eye. The wound in his thigh looked bad, as though he had been – well... stabbed. Helena was no expert in such matters, as there were very few duels fought in these parts, but she knew fish knives, and that looked like a stab with a dagger.

Its jagged edges left raw red skin around the wound, and the struggle that he had surely suffered to sail here, perhaps from France, and the short journey he had just taken from shipwreck to safety had torn again at the injury.

There was nothing for it. Helena grimaced, and took off her greatcoat as she realised just what she needed to do.

"Sir," she began, pulling up her sodden blonde hair with a few extra pins that she took from the side. "Sir, your injury is very bad, and if it is not cleaned and patched, then it could become infected."

Nothing but a groan was her reply. Helena rolled her eyes. Never before had she acted as a Good Samaritan, and now she could see why.

It took almost five minutes to heave up onto the sofa, and another two to rid him, and here she could not but blush, of the britches that he wore. She was forced to cut them off as her fingers hesitated to reach towards those buttons that a young lady always saw, but never touched. He did not prevent her; from the fluttering of his eyes, he was bouncing between conscious and unconsciousness anyway.

Helena moved around the house almost silently, collecting the items that she would need: the bottle of rum that they kept for emergencies, a fishing wire, a curved embroidery needle. This had been a skill, sadly, that Helena had learned from a young age and which had come in useful more than twice a year. A fisherman's life was precarious, after all, and a slip on the boat or an unplanned flick of the wrist, and many a man had come to Mrs Thatcher, and then to her assistant, Miss Metcalfe, for help.

"Now then, sir," Helena murmured in what she hoped was her most comforting voice. Usually she knew the name of the man she was to help, and they knew what she was about to do. It helped steady the nerves. Tonight, as the gale stormed around her little house, her father miles hence at the Anchor, rum would have to suffice.

"Pierre," came a faint voice from the man, and for a moment his eyes opened and looked directly into hers.

Helena almost flinched at the intensity of that gaze: simultaneously both warm and cold, a deep and serious look. It made her feel as though she was the only woman on earth.

"H-Helena," she replied finally, and smiled weakly. "Well, Pierre, I am going to knit back together this wound you have, to help with the healing. I will use a little rum to clean it, and then a little down your throat to keep you still. Do you understand?"

He had not moved. There seemed to be no strength to raise his head or even shake it, but he did whisper, "*Oui Mademoiselle Helene, je comprends.*"

Helena swallowed. The men she usually worked on were old, old before their time, but at least twenty years older than herself. This gentleman was in the full flush of youth, and could not be more than five years older than herself, and she barely twenty. His legs were long, strong but shaking now with the pain.

All she had to do was think of him as a patient, nothing more. Even a leg, just a leg. That was all she needed to do.

The candle was brought down from the windowsill, a little rum was poured down Pierre's neck, a little around the wound, and Helena threaded the needle. She was ready.

To his credit, he barely flinched as the needle went in. Helena worked as quickly as she could, murmuring slowly under her breath as though it were a spell to keep him quiet and still: "There we are, almost done, you are doing well, thank you Pierre for remaining so still, and I am coming back round, and soon it will be finished..."

It felt like an age. Her feet were still damp and her stomach growled at least once from the hunger that had sent her out into the dark in the first place, but she concentrated hard. Never before had she done a bad job, not since Mrs Thatcher had trusted her to take the needle, and she was blowed if she was going to be overwhelmed by these slightly strange circumstances.

And then it was over, and she was saying, "There,

Monsieur Pierre, it is all done. I will just get some britches of my father's for you, and we can...I mean, you can change."

Her face flushed. She knew very well that under that scanty piece of cloth that she had left after cutting the britches away was...well, that private part of a man. Undergarments were rarely worn by men of any social standing, and that meant that mere inches from her fingers had been –

"I will get them now," she said hastily, and almost ran to the narrow stairway.

Halfway up them, she stopped, and leaned against the wall for support, hand clutched to her breast.

What had she done? What was she doing? If anyone came to call at this moment – unlikely as that was, considering the weather and the time which must be gone nine o'clock – then what would they find?

A half-naked man in her house, and her father away, that is what. Helena's face burned at the thought of it. And not just a half-naked man: a half-naked, handsome, Frenchman.

Helena closed her eyes, and tried not to remember the feeling of that strong, hairy muscle underneath her searching fingers. She had concentrated on the injury, yes, but she could not help her mind wandering further upwards to what was hidden from her. He was so handsome, there was no denying it.

He had remained still and quiet as she had worked, and those lips had barely moved. To kiss those lips, to have that jaw pronounce her name –

Helena started, and found herself still standing halfway up the stairs, leaning against the wall, eyes closed. Her cheeks burned, and they were still burning as she made her way back down the stairs after retrieving a pair of britches from her father's room.

But before she walked into the parlour, she stopped. She could hear a voice: it was Pierre, and he sounded wretched.

"...Giselle...Giselle..."

A flare of something that tasted like jealousy rushed through Helena's body, and she started at it. What right did she have to be jealous? This gentleman was a stranger to her, and she had no claim on him. He belonged to this Giselle lady, and she should think no more of him.

Mind resolved, she strode through into the room and smiled briefly at him.

"Well, Pierre, I think it is best if you try to sleep here tonight. I do not think that it is a good idea to attempt the removal of you to my father's room."

He smiled at her, and her heart thumped. And then he said, "I am a criminal, you know."

The heart that had been thumping came to an abrupt stop.

Pierre nodded lazily, though that could have been the aftereffects of the rum. "*Mais oui*, a criminal of France. I have escaped, petite mademoiselle, and you are hiding me, and for that, I thank you."

For a moment, Helena thought that she would be unable to find her tongue. Eventually, she said, "I am not hiding you, I am sheltering you."

At once she felt the foolishness of her words: did it make any difference, really?

And Pierre was smiling at her, and she could not help but notice how it brightened his face and gave it even more strength and beauty. "Nay, mademoiselle Helene, you are my saviour, *mon sauveteur*. You have my thanks."

She stared at him, in equal measure repulsed and

intrigued. What had he done, this handsome Frenchman who evidently was born of one of the noblest families? What brought him here, fleeing his country – fleeing justice?

And what was she to do with him?

~

*P*ierre almost grinned when he saw the reaction on the lovely woman's face: a mixture of horror, awe, and interest.

Well, so it always was. We simply cannot help it, he thought hazily as he watched the woman attempt to find something to say. We are curious – and the English far more so than the French, *naturellement*.

"I will...I will let you put on your britches," were the words that Helena, that was her name, eventually spoke. "Sleep well, *monsieur Pierre*."

Her accent was light, and yet the strong English tint flowed through it. Pierre wanted to smile at it, but his body seemed to be moving in slow motion.

"Thank you, mademoiselle, but you have forgotten my drink," he said, looking at the little table that was empty, save for the end of the fishing wire.

Helena's beautiful mouth became a taut line. "I have forgotten your drink?"

Pierre nodded, and then stopped quickly as it started to make the room tilt a little to the left, and spin. "Oui, mademoiselle, I must have a drink. Perhaps the rum?"

He had half meant it as a joke, to tell the truth, but when he saw the way that her eyes widened, he said hastily, "Or some tea, or coffee, anything really, for I am – I think the word is, *parchet?*"

She stared at him for a moment. By God, but she was beautiful: the English rose that he had heard so much about, but had barely believed when those who had travelled to this isle had returned. The earrings that had dazzling his eyes were shimmering now in the candlelight. White blonde hair, shimmering in the little light the candle created, soft white skin, pale now due to fear if he were any judge, and that rosebud mouth, pink and pert and just ready for him to –

His whole body flexed, and that was when he realised that his britches were gone – and certain parts of him almost open to the air.

"*Mon pantalon!*" He cried, glancing down and then glancing back at her, furious. "What have you – you witch, those were fifty francs!"

Pierre stared at her in dismay, and attempted to ignore the way her dripping hair was starting to make her gown damp. He had not noticed that before; but then, who does notice these sorts of details in a mere servant?

"I think I just saved your life," the woman said coolly. "If I had left you out there," and here she paused, glancing at the window for effect which was still being lashed with rain, "then there is every chance you would have drowned come morning, or died of exposure, or infection to your leg. You should be thanking me on bended knee – at least, when you can."

His stare widened. How dare she speak to him like that: like they were equals, like she had any claim to his better nature! There was a heady mixture of gentleness and fire within her, and he watched the struggle of it in those perfect features until gentleness won out.

"My...my apologies, sir," she said stiffly, and she moved through a door which he assumed was to a kitchen, and was proved right when she returned with a glass filled with a cloudy golden liquid. "Here is your drink. I think the rum would go a little to your head, but that is cider, and will perform the twin roles of keeping you from thirst, and take you towards sleep."

Helene – for that was how he thought of her, he could not help it – kneeled by his head, and gently tilted the glass to his lips, bringing her other hand to his head to raise him up. Her touch was soft, gentle, caressing. Perhaps he was imagining that last one. She was very pretty, almost glowing now that he was this close to her.

"I shall place it here," putting it down on the little table that occupied the middle of the room. "'Tis but a short distance from you, and if you require it in the night, you should be able to reach it. Now, goodnight."

Pierre stared at her. So, despite thinking him a criminal, and a French one at that – he was not ignorant of the way the English taught their daughters – she had brought him a drink. Had wished him a goodnight. What did that mean?

Before he was able to open his mouth to say anything, she had gone.

No matter. He was not going anywhere fast, if the ache in his leg was any indication, and he would speak with her in the morning.

Sighing, he stretched out on the sofa and attempted to ignore the twinge in his thigh each time he moved. He would have plenty of time to explain things in the morning, after all. When you are Pierre d'Épiluçon, a nobleman of France, no matter what any revolution said, you learned to bide your time.

And in any case, he would rather have a little more strength the next time that he saw mademoiselle Helene. She intrigued him as no woman ever had before. Every other lady of his acquaintance between the age of fifteen and fifty had preened and prattled at the mere sight of him, back home in France.

Pierre smiled ruefully as he slowly removed the ruined britches, and placed the borrowed ones on – rough and poor quality though they were. He had always thought that the simpering and the sighing had been due to his features: his handsome face, his tall strength, the wit of his tongue.

But place him for five minutes with an Englishwoman who knew naught of his name nor his riches, and it was plain that those were the true attractions that he had waved under the noses of so many eligible young ladies.

He sighed, and pulled the blanket that had been placed beside him over his body. He was no longer cold, but strangely cold and shivering. The coarseness of the blanket startled him as he drew it up to his face; never before had he suffered through such mean quality. To think that this time yesterday, he was asleep in his own bed with silk sheets, and not a care in the world.

Well, almost none. He had known his wealth had been considered a crime by French society for a while. He had been foolish not to expect this. but he could explain that in the morning to the gentle and yet fiery mademoiselle Helene. Perhaps there was even more to her than already met the eye.

3

The gale had dissipated long before Helena opened her eyes again, but it was yet another loud crash that awoke her.

She sat up bolt upright, and listened eagerly for a continuation of the noise, but all was silent. Bright sunlight was pouring through the gaps in her curtains, and there was an unnatural stillness in the air.

Then, "*Merde.* Why cannot they keep this place in better order?"

Helena's eyes widened. For a brief moment, she had almost forgotten the adventures of the night before: the hunger that had driven her outside, the unexpected bounty the sea had offered, the struggle to get him home, the knife wound, the rum –

The criminal.

"Why can't I walk, *stupide!*"

Another cry echoed through the house, and Helena sighed. There was no use in her staying her, in her warm comfortable bed, even if the clock had not just struck six.

Throwing off her bed covers and grabbing a dressing

gown to cover her nightdress, Helena pattered down the well-worn stairs, and almost screamed at the sight that met her eyes at the bottom.

Pierre d'Épiluçon, wearing no shirt and barely keeping his britches up, was covered in what looked like blood, and was staggering around the room with a dazed look on his face, mumbling under his breath.

"Pierre!" She breathed, staring at him with concerned eyes. "*Monsieur*, are you hurt?"

The stumbling figure stopped, and turned to face her. It smiled vaguely.

"*Bonjour*," he muttered quietly, not quite looking at her but at the mantlepiece to her right. "*Et qu'elle beau jour il était!*"

Helena took a step forward. He did not seem to be in a violent mood, just a strange one: he could certainly not be overly hot for it was cold in this room now that the fire had died down in the night – and yet perspiration seemed to pour from every inch of his body.

"*Monsieur*, why do not you sit down?" Helena said quietly as she took another step into the room. "You must be tired after your ordeal, after all, and you should rest and gather your strength."

Pierre smiled at her. "Giselle?"

It was difficult not to feel a slight irritation here, but Helena took another step forward, and peered at the gentleman closely.

It was not blood. It was rum. Somehow, the stupid man had managed to pour rum all down himself, and when it met the dark brown coarse britches of her father that she had lent him, it had crusted and dried, and looked remarkably like his wound had opened up again.

"Giselle, why so quiet?"

Helena tried desperately not to roll her eyes. Well then, he was drunk: though how he managed to be so intoxicated at this early hour was anyone's guess. Was this typical for a Frenchman? Did they have rum for breakfast?

Something touched her arm, and she jumped, looking wildly into Pierre's face. There were beads of sweat on his brow, and his eyes looked mazed.

"I think I am dreaming," he whispered darkly. "For I know that I am in France, and yet this does not feel like France, *n'est-ce pas*?"

His hand was burned around her wrist, and yet it was not the fervent heat of love, but the toxic heat of fever. Helena placed her other hand on his forehead: yes, he was burning up, and almost certainly delirious from the fever.

It still did not explain the rum, but it was a start.

"Come now, monsieur," she said gently, taking his hand from her arm and retaining it as a sort of rudder, attempting to steer him. "Let us take you back to the sofa, and you can lie down."

"But the butler is waiting for me," complained Pierre in dazed tones. "I am required to approve the latest shoot, and without me nothing can begin."

Helena almost tripped over the small table as she tried to move him forward, and he took two jaggedy steps, and then stopped.

"Giselle, is this a dream?" Pierre stared at her with confused and hurting eyes, but there was a glaze across them that told Helena she had been right: it was a fever. "It feels so real, and yet, *tu sais*, you cannot be here. So what is it?"

"It is a dream," said Helena firmly as she gently forced him to sit on the sofa. First things first. Poor soul, it was impossible to know just how long he had spent in that boat trying to find the shore: dehydration, exposure, and fever all whirled through her mind. "But in this dream, you have to wear a shirt. Where is yours?"

Pierre gazed up at her with a content expression on his face. Apparently, being told that you were in a dream was rather comforting.

"I see no reason to exert myself any further," he remarked lazily, in almost a complete return to his old self. He lay back on the sofa, and slowly raised his legs, stiff as his injured one was, onto the sofa. "After all, this is a dream, *n'est pas*? So nothing I do here has any real consequence. Therefore, I can do nothing."

Helena rolled her eyes. How incredibly like a wealthy man to assume such things.

"Fine," she said, irritably, remembering that she had not eaten in almost fifteen hours. "I will find it myself – and then it is breakfast for me, and cold water for you."

He began to murmur something on the lines that surely in a dream, his butler could send over a brace of partridges, but Helena had already departed to the kitchen.

She had almost completely buttered a thin slice of bread, not a truly arduous task, when a shout rent the air.

"What is it – what has happened?" She gasped as she ran through into the parlour, dressing gown flapping open in her haste.

Pierre was huddled at one end of the sofa, pointing at nothing at all, and shouting wildly, "*L'anglais*! Quick, men, to your pistols, the enemy is upon us!"

Helena rushed forwards, and he started, eyes wide.

"Giselle? Mon Dieu, what are you doing here, this is no place for a lady?"

She stared at him helplessly. When a fever took over a mind, she knew, it could take it to the strangest of places, but usually it drank all strength from the person too, so their delirious wanderings were quiet, still, unobtrusive.

Not so with Pierre d'Épiluçon, obviously. His strength had remained, had fought back from the muddles of the mind, leaving her with a man unsure of where he was, but still strong enough to knock her down, if he chose.

Helene had not looked in on her father's bedroom when she had rushed down to attend to the first noise that had awoken her, because she did not need to. She knew the moods that her father talked himself into, and besides, if he had come home last night, he would probably have discovered Pierre asleep on the sofa. Even if he had been missed, the shouting of this morning would have been enough to wake up.

So then, she was alone. Alone with a Frenchman who seemed convinced that he was about to be attacked by the English.

Well, he was not wrong.

"Sit down soldier!" She barked, glaring at him with the best military look that she could muster, and probably approximating something more like constipated. It did not matter, however: it was what Pierre thought that mattered. "I have never seen such a raggedy man in all my life. Where is your shirt, soldier?"

For a moment, Helena was unsure whether it had worked. There was so much confusion in his eyes, his poor overheated mind telling him so much, that she was not sure exactly whether her words would even reach him.

And then he sat up straight on the sofa, and tried to salute. His hand went flying behind his head, but it was evidently clear what it was supposed to be.

"Shirt – shirt lost, *monsieur*," he said smartly, eyes not quite focused on her.

Helena grabbed at one of her father's old shirts, sat in the corner on the mending pile. "Then place this over your head, monsieur, and lie down. You are injured."

It took twenty minutes to get Pierre to lie down calmly, and a further ten to sit with him quietly to send him into the land of sleep. She watched his eyes flutter madly underneath their lids, even when his breathing had slowed to a gentle pace.

It was only now, in the light of the new day, that she was able to take a proper look at him. Last night she had only gained impressions, ideas of what he looked like, but now that she could examine him with leisure, she could see that most of her ideas had been correct.

Strong. Strength was almost chiselled into every piece of him, and if she had not been sure of that, all she had to do was take her memory back half an hour, when he was wandering the house without a shirt on.

Hair cropped short, shorter than any English style. Perhaps it was the French one. A jawline that was strong, but a mouth that seemed kind.

Helena blushed. She may not have said a word, but the thoughts were enough.

She sat with him for another five minutes, and saw with relief that his breathing did seem to have slowed to a gentle sleep.

Her stomach rumbled. It was time for food, but no sooner has she risen from the chair that she had pulled to the sofa, did he stir.

"Giselle? Do not leave me, *mon petit...*"

Helena sighed, and dropped to the seat once more. It appeared that she was going to go without food for the present; the longer that he slept, the quicker the fever would break, and she could not be sure that she would be quite able to restrain him with words next time he was convinced of falsehoods again.

The hours drifted by. Helena seemed to move beyond hunger and out the other side, and the few times that she attempted to rise and get herself a drink, a hand would shoot out and try to keep her there.

Whether he was asleep or not, she concluded, her presence was clearly felt, and she could do no more than remain with him.

Around one o'clock, feelings of quiet resentment started to grow in her heart, ignore them though she might. It was all very well, she thought, for Pierre to wish her to stay, but she must eat at sometime! It was nigh on an entire day that she had been without sustenance, and –

"Mama?"

It was more of a breath than a word, and Helena started to hear such softness from the hulk of a man lying on her sofa. She leaned forward, but said nothing.

Pierre's eyes were closed, but he was frowning as though slightly displeased with what he saw. "Mama, where are you going?"

His voice was not pleading, or whining, but concerned. The frown deepened.

"No, Mama, I told you not to go there, 'tis *dangereux*," he whispered, the frown tugging at his eyebrows and a crease appearing on his forehead.

"What do you mean, Papa is dead?"

Helena's jaw dropped open, and she stared in horror at the man who seemed to be reliving some of the most desperate moments of his life. His jaw was tight, as though refusing to believe what the apparition before him was saying.

"*Non,* I do not believe it," he whispered. "Papa escaped,

did not we receive his letter? Why are you saying such things – *c'est des mensonges*, all lies!"

His hand was moving frantically in her direction, and she grasped at it, holding it tightly.

The frown disappeared, and a sad smile instead covered his cheeks. "Ah, Giselle. We are the only ones left. We must run, hide – there is nowhere in France they will not find it, *tu comprends?*"

Understanding was now beginning to dawn in Helena's mind, but it was not happy knowledge. She, like all others in Europe, had heard about the terrible events in France over the last few years, but they had always been something far off: something that was happening to other people, nothing for her to be concerned with.

And yet now, here before her lay a very real victim of *la révolution*. A man who apparently lost his parents; lost them to *madame guillotine*.

And what of this Giselle? Was she a sister, a friend, a lover? Clearly she was someone that Pierre cared about, someone he wanted to be safe.

Where was she now?

"Ah, Giselle, I do not know," Pierre replied fretfully to an unasked question. "I cannot find their bodies, and so the burial must wait. Ah, I am so alone!"

Helena's heart, perhaps icy due to the lack of food, thawed instantly to hear some bereaved tones. The horror of that time could not be taken in, but she had to know more.

"Pierre," she whispered in a low voice. "Who is Giselle? Where is she?"

At the name, his eyes moved towards her, though still closed. "Giselle?"

Helena nodded, and then realising the stupidity of that action, whispered, "Yes."

For a moment, he made no sound or movement. Then, "Giselle, we must run – we must flee France! But where to go; Italy is too far, and Spain its own disaster. Perhaps to England? *Oui? Non?*"

"Was she," and here Helena had to swallow down the horror of the question, but she had to know. "Was she in the boat with you, Pierre?"

"A boat, a boat, *mais oui,* we shall require a boat," muttered Pierre under his breath, and he turned in whatever kind of sleep he was in to face the back of the sofa. "And how much will you sell yours for, *gentils messieurs?*"

"Where are you from?" Helena asked urgently. "Where were you trying to get to – do you have friends in England?"

"No friends, just subjects," Pierre replied with a little giggle. "I am from nowhere, and yet everywhere. No cage can hold me, *c'est vrai,* but I am a little tied up right now..."

His giggles dissolved into snores, and he fell into what sounded like a genuine restful sleep.

Helena leaned back in her chair, and shook her head. There was no use trying to get any sense out of him at this moment. She would have to be patient, and hope that the delirium would dissipate soon.

But then, she thought as she leaned back into the comforting embrace of the armchair, what if the fever had caught hold of him before he entered this house? What if Giselle does not even exist? What if his mention of being a criminal – so shocking to hear late last night – were also a part of that delirium?

Helena rubbed her eyes, trying to ignore the gnawing feeling in her stomach. As she crossed her legs under her nightgown, her feet touched something strange. Peering down, she saw Pierre's brocade embroidered jacket that had been unceremoniously thrown down earlier.

She bit her lip. It was not wrong to look, after all. She was his guardian, and the more that she knew about him, surely, the better.

It took less than three seconds to lift the jacket up and start to rifle through the pockets. She did so silently, glancing at the unmoving figure on the sofa to check that he was still asleep. Her fingers brushed against something cold, and she drew it out.

Not for the first time that day, her jaw fell open. A long chain of pearls had dribbled out of the pocket, and tangled into one end, a diamond brooch.

She checked more carefully now, and found sovereigns, francs, another necklace, this time made of gold with a ruby pendant, and a good number of cravats made of the softest silk she had ever touched.

Helena pooled the treasure in her lap and stared at it. Well. No hint at an identity, but he was certainly rich.

The temptation to awaken him and ask more serious questions threatened to overwhelm her, but she pushed it away. Peering over him, Helena could clearly see that Pierre was, at last, relaxed and peaceful.

It would be wrong to satisfy her own curiosity in that way. She would have to be patient, and wait for the fever to break.

She sighed, and reached over to the little table where a letter she had received the day before was still resting. She had not time to read it yesterday, what with one thing and another, and now was the perfect opportunity to indulge in a little news from her sister.

Dearest Helena,

My pen has hardly known where to start, my dearest one, and yet I shall put it down to parchment at last to tell you the most incredible news – news that I have longed, one day, to write you with, but had never expected such an early occasion to be so merry.

My sister: I am to be married.

I know it will shock you, as you are unaware of my acquaintance in general here in London, and I have given you no cause for suspicion as no name has dropped into my letters frequently enough for you to suspect.

All has changed. My life is not what it is was, and I am now engaged to Alexander, the Duke of Caershire.

Helena could not help but gasp at this point, and drop the letter down into her lap as she gazed through the window.

Alexander, the Duke of Caershire. The Duke of Caershire! But that would mean – surely, there could be no other consequence than...

Yes. I am to be the Duchess of Caershire. It hardly seems real, I will admit, but Caershire informs me that I must better get accustomed to answering to such a ridiculous title, and of course, I am sure that I will.

It is difficult to remember, Helena, that but one week ago, I did not know him. Those who say that love only comes on in stages are liars, for I cannot tell you how rapidly he gained my affections.

He makes me so happy, Lenny. If he were but a pauper, I think we could be happy, but I write in haste – and will tell the complete story in a thicker and less frantic letter, near drowning in the Thames and all – in tell you that we will be doing absolutely anything in our power to help you. Caershire is not currently aware of any vacant properties on the Loxwich estate, but as soon as one is found, you and Father will come

and live in it. You shall want for nothing, and Father will no
longer have to sink his sore and aging hands into the ocean to
feed you.

I must go – the wedding preparations are in earnest! I will
write again soon with dates, and a carriage will be sent.

For I am, until then, your dearest sister,

Teresa

Helena read the letter twice more through, once in haste, and the third time with careful study.

So. She was to be the sister-in-law of a Duke! The weight that had forced her down was suddenly lifted, and it felt almost possible that she would rise off the chair and start to float to the ceiling!

Could anyone have predicted such a turn of events? That Teresa Metcalfe, poor middle child of a ruined gentleman, forced to go to London and act as the courtesan to the nobility, will now become one herself?

Helena's smile faltered slightly. It was unseemly of her to admit, of course, the small yet sharp pang of jealousy that wrenched through her heart. Teresa had borne much, to be sure, to keep their family afloat in different times, but had not she, Helena, also suffered? Had she not been left alone with their father, forced to mend and cook and clean like a scullery maid, with little thanks and no praise?

She shook her head. This was nonsense talk: the success of one sister would bring prosperity to both, she had no fear of anything but that.

Placing the letter, jewels and jewellery into the small box underneath the sofa that she kept for her own personal treasures, it was only when Helena leaned back into the chair again that she saw Pierre d'Épiluçon's eye staring at her.

4

$\mathcal{T}$he ground did not seem to be moving any more, but that was of little comfort.

Pierre raised a hand to his head, and was somewhat relieved to discover that not only could he find his hand, but it could find his head. It hurt. He seemed drenched with something – rain? Ocean? Sweat? He could not tell.

It was only then that he became conscious that attached to his head was a body. It felt awful: chilled to the bone, with every limb wrung out like a wet towel.

What had happened? Where was he?

He opened his eyes.

At first, his sight struggled to take in exactly what he was seeing. It was so unlike what his mind had expected to view, so the lightly patterned wallpaper and old sofa on which he lounged faded in and out of view.

The grogginess of his head seemed to come into stronger focus, however, when he blinked, and then some of the memories – or the dream he had been having – came back to him.

Sailing – no, shipwrecked. Shipwrecked on an English

shore, on English sand. And an English woman? Or had that been Giselle? The images, blurred and hazy, swam in and out of view of his mind's eye, and Pierre closed his eyes in the attempt to concentrate.

And then they snapped open again. No, it had been real: he had escaped France, he knew it, and now he was in England. Where exactly, he did not know. With whom, he had just as little comprehension.

"Ah, you are awake then."

A vision: a woman, simply dressed in a light pink gown, holding what looked like manna from heaven.

"'Tis only a little rainwater, I confess," said the golden-haired dream. "But it seemed a pity to waste it, and you were in need of water badly. Here."

Without waiting for his permission to approach, she continued forward and kneeled by the sofa on which Pierre lay. Before he could say a word with his dropped jaw, she cupped his head and gently poured water down his throat.

It was the sweetest draught he had ever tasted. His parched throat burned slightly at the contact, but was instantly soothed, and his mind started to clear.

"Hel-Helene?"

She smiled, and Pierre gazed, completely captivated by her smile. It was beyond beauty: it was a heady mixture of unconscious pleasure to hear her name from his lips, and the joy that it sprang in his soul, and the curve of her pink lips, and the softness of her touch, and it grabbed at his heart as none of the *Dames* of the French court ever had.

"Helene," he repeated as she took the cup away, and smiled quietly at him. "That is your name, *n'est-ce pas*?"

She nodded. "Helena, but I suppose it is much the same. And yours is Pierre – Pierre d'Épiluçon?"

Something in his stomach jolted when she attempted to wrap her tongue around his name. "Pierre d'Épiluçon."

Helena leaned back and rested her head against the chair. "Well, *Monsieur Pierre*, I regret to inform you that you have been unwell."

Pierre tried to sit up, and found that he could do so as long as he did not move too fast. "Unwell?"

She nodded, and the sunlight pouring through the window behind him made her hair beam. "I...I found you on the beach, not twenty yards from this house. You had been shipwrecked, I think, and struggled to find your way. You did not seem unwell, but when I awoke I found you in a fever."

"A fever?" Pierre stared at her, and tried to remember. Well, that would certainly make sense. How could Giselle have been here, after all – and his parents, he had talked with them...but they could not have been here, it was not possible.

Helena seemed to be watching him closely. Suddenly conscious that there may be a tear creeping into his eye, Pierre forced himself to twist on the sofa and drop his feet down to the floor. His shoes were gone, but a pair of what looked like ancient slippers were waiting for him.

"It has been but one day," Helena gently lifted each foot and placed it in a slipper, "and I must admit, I am relieved to see that the fever has broken. If it had continued much further, I would have had need to call Mrs Thatcher."

This last name meant nothing to Pierre, so he brushed it aside, asking, "But you, *mademoiselle Helene*. You have taken care of me?"

He could see the answer immediately in the modest glow of recognition, but all she said was, "I was here, and I made you comfortable. I am no doctor, *monsieur*."

"*Non*, but I feel much better!" Pierre tried a smile, and found that his winning charm did not seem to have been damped by his drop in the ocean. "That would have taken a little skill, I would say. I am in your debt, mademoiselle – at least, I assume that it is *mademoiselle*. Should I say, *madame*?"

The young woman stared at him for a moment, and Pierre was surprised to find within himself a desperate hope that he was wrong. But how could he be: a gentle woman like she, beautiful, caring, all alone in this house, small as it was? These slippers were not made for a woman's feet.

"I-I am unmarried, monsieur," she eventually said, with colour in her cheeks. "Why would you think otherwise?"

Pierre smiled, and this was a genuine smile, born of relief and a little heat that flooded through his heart. "You are alone here, mademoiselle, without anyone?"

He regretted his phrasing at once, for he saw in an instant that she took it as a threat.

"My father is – is in town," she said stiffly, rising and moving towards what Pierre assumed was the kitchen. It was so difficult to navigate in these peasant homes. "I assure you, I am quite protected, and what's more there are three more cottages but a mile from – "

"*Pardon,* you misunderstand me," said Pierre hastily, outstretching a placatory hand. "I just wished to enquire whether there were any more of the house to whom I owed the gratitude of saving my life."

He almost overdid it, he could see that in the colour of her cheeks, but she was mollified.

Helena stepped forward, cup still in hand. "Well then," she spoke with a little discomfort, but less distrust. "In that case, you should have some more water. You need to regain your strength."

Her hips swayed slightly as she walked towards him, and

Pierre discovered that regaining strength was not going to be a problem. Controlling the strength of desire that Helena was starting to awake in him was going to be a very different matter.

She watched him with those blue eyes as he drank, unaided this time. And then she spoke, causing him to splutter into the cup. "Who is Giselle?"

"Giselle?" He coughed, trying to breathe as she took the cup hastily from him. "What do you mean, Giselle?"

Helena sat back in the chair, staring at him with a far more knowing look than he was comfortable with. No one in France had ever looked at him like that. "Giselle. You mentioned her several times during your delirium; you called out to her a few times, if I recall. Who is she?"

Pierre shifted on the sofa, conscious of the red tint that was starting to diffuse over his cheeks. So, he had called out for her – it was truly embarrassing to be caught in such feeling by someone as strikingly beautiful as Miss Helena.

"Forget my request," she said unexpectedly, and the eyes he had dropped rose quickly to meet hers. "I should not have asked, I had no right to pry."

She handed him the bowl that she had brought through from the kitchen, and Pierre stared down at it, horrified. He had never seen anything like it in his life, and hoped to God that he never would again.

"What is this?"

Helena smiled mischievously. "Why, monsieur, are you telling me that you have never eaten English gruel before?"

Pierre picked up the spoon that had almost drowned in the bowl, and watched as something grey, lumpy, and warm dribbled down back into the mass. "This is food?"

She laughed, and picked up her own bowl – a bowl, Pierre saw, that was filled with a very different fare. "'Tis the very lifeblood of English schools and prisons, monsieur, and there will be those who tell you that they are essentially the same place. No, I jest sir, 'tis food. Something plain and simple, to bear you up after your fever. You can enjoy real food in time."

"Real food like that?"

Helena smiled down at her own bowl. "Yes, fish stew. It is delicious, fresh from the sea that I pulled it from a few hours ago, and it is not for you until you have finished your own."

Pierre grimaced, but lowered the spoon. Anything to keep off the topic of Giselle.

He was not so fortunate.

"I think," said his fair companion, hesitantly, "that you lost your family in the Revolution. Is that true?"

Unable to tell whether it was a blessing or a curse that his mouth was now full of gruel, Pierre nodded, and swallowed. "I appreciate that you have no wish to force the truth from me, so I shall give it to you. My father was *guillotined,* my mother killed by a mob, and my sister – Giselle – tried to escape to England a year ago."

Helena's own spoon had paused halfway between her bowl and her mouth, and fish stew was dripping. "Guillotined? Killed? Your mother?"

Pierre nodded again. "I have not heard from my sister in that year, and when I received news that my neck was the next to be laid on the line for France, I knew that it was time for me to come and look for her myself. Letters, servants, rewards could not bring me joy. And I can never go back now: France is as closed to me, for the rest of my days."

She was staring at him, and the horror and compassion that mingled across her face was painful for Pierre to see. "I am so sorry for your loss, monsieur, it is – well, it is simply terrible."

Pierre swallowed. "It...it was terrible. Sometimes I dream about them, and it is so real that when I wake up, I almost forget that it is happened. And then I remember, and it is like going through the bereavement all over again."

They eat in silence for a minute, and then Helena peered at him curiously. "You did tell me, monsieur, that you were a criminal. Why did you lie?"

He laughed, setting down the almost empty bowl. "In a way, it was the truth. I and my kind have been considered outlaws, criminals, poison to the country of France, all for the crime of being rich in coffers and rich in bloodline."

"That is awful!" Helena's mouth was aghast, and his spirit soared to see her so outraged. "Pierre, that is despicable, how can it be allowed?"

"Do not fret yourself," he said in his best reassuring tone, reaching out to take her hand. It was warm, and it sparked something in him that he could not describe. "These troubles of mine, and my people – they are something that you, in your state of life, will never have to know anything of. 'Tis just for those of us burdened with nobility."

～

*H*elena felt the heat and irritation rush through her body, and her cheeks coloured. "And what exactly is that supposed to mean?"

She could see by the surprise in his eyes that Pierre had not been expecting such a rush of fierce emotion.

"*Pardon?*"

"Burdened with nobility?" She repeated, trying to maintain her composure but failing miserably. "It may surprise you to learn, *monsieur,* that my family was once relatively wealthy. We owned much of the land around here, and if it had not been for some…unfortunate financial decisions that my father made, along with familial sickness, well, I would have left you under the care and charge of my housekeeper."

Helena saw with sadness that Pierre was attempting not to smile.

"Ah, you may smile, sir," she said quietly, the gentleness that was truly at the core of her soul washing over her and quelling the fiery sparks of anger, "but I can inform you that I received news just yesterday that my sister is engaged to be married to the Duke of Caershire. I am not, perhaps, to be a duchess myself, but to be the sister of one should, I am sure, make me quite as noble as many."

She had not known exactly what she was to expect from these words: she was certainly delighted to be able to speak them, proud of her sister, honoured with the newly formed connection. What she had not excepted was for Pierre d'Épiluçon's eyes to widen, soften, and then settle in a new expression of respect and interest – and, and here she coloured slightly, with desire.

"And there you show your true colours," she said quietly. "Yes, I see how you look at me now. I scorn your idea of nobility, if it can have such a change in your view of a person. Am I not the same woman who saved your life? Do you not owe me the same respect?"

Pierre may have been born a noble, but at that moment, he looked unable to speak. "*Pardon, je suis désolé* – it was not my intention to…"

Helena was not trying to glare, but she could not help it. "Perhaps, monsieur, you need to learn to view people as worth something beyond their social status."

5

*I*t was a day of frustration for Pierre d'Épiluçon, as he sat on the sofa, not permitted to move or stir by his hostess, when he felt with every passing moment that his energy and vitality was returning to him.

The sun moved slowly and lazily across the room, adding to the atmosphere of futility. Pierre fidgeted, and received nothing but stern looks all the morning from Helena.

"Sit still," she would say quietly. "You must regain your strength."

And so he did. Nothing moved save his eyes, but they found more and more to be pleased with as the days progressed, for he found the bustle of Helena more than enough entertainment to keep his mind alive.

At first, he tried to ignore her as she pottered about the room: moving to the mending pile, quickly stitching together a shirt, moving then to the kitchen and bringing through some spring flowers in a vase, popping upstairs for a shawl. It was as though she was unable to keep still, unwilling to stay in one place.

Unable to accept his gaze?

Pierre felt longing flow through him as he watched her. True, he had noticed her quiet and still beauty the moment that he had taken a good look at her, but it was only now that he watched her that he noticed her elegance, her attention to detail, the way she cared for that little house as though it was a person. The earrings that she always wore, diamonds they looked like, though he supposed now they were but glass, glimmering in the light.

And then three days after he had arrived, she broke into his thoughts. "Do you require anything?"

Pierre started, and his gaze focused on her, standing before him, hands on those flowing hips.

He swallowed. "*Non, merci mademoiselle.*"

She moved away again, but not before giving him an arch look that made parts of him stir that really should not be awakened, as a twinge from his leg reminded him of his recent injury.

Now she was moving through the room, dusting. It was incredible, Pierre mused as he watched the turn of her neck as she looked around at her work, just how elegantly and neatly she kept the place, considering their circumstances.

"You watch me, sir." Her words were not sharp, but her look was. "Do I displease you?"

"Quite the contrary," he responded without thinking, and almost laughed aloud at the blush that his words instigated. "My apologies, mademoiselle, I only meant that you are doing nothing to incite displeasure. Please, continue as though I am not here."

And yet he could hardly forget that she was there. After lunch, she gave him a small book – the only book that he had noticed in the house – and he looked down with pleasure to see that it was Voltaire.

"Ah, Voltaire!" He smiled at her, and was glad to see a small smile in return. "I did not know that you were an aficionado of Voltaire!"

For a moment, she rested on the armchair beside him, and now there was a natural smile. "Yes, he was my favourite author. When I was small, we had a library with his complete works, but...well, all the books had to be sold. That was the only one I was permitted to keep, and that only because we had a duplicate."

Pierre looked at her gently, and reached out a hand to clasp hers. It jolted more desire in him than he knew what to do with. "Helene, I am sure that one day, you will have your own library."

Helena looked up at him, and his jaw dropped at the longing he saw in her eyes. Yes, she felt the same pull, the same –

"I would love a library of my own," she said wistfully, and all the hopes that had risen within him died away. "But I suppose I shall visit my sister's, once she is married to the Duke of Caershire."

And without another word, she pulled away and disappeared once more into the kitchen.

Pierre sank back into the sofa, trying to catch his breath. Well, if he had hoped to convince himself that he felt nothing for her, then he was sadly mistaken! Fire was flooding through his body like never before, and if he was not careful, he would be in some danger of regarding Miss – but then, he did not know her full name.

The afternoon dragged on with Pierre forbidden, continuously, from stirring an inch. He watched her, and saw the truth in her that her family had once been wealthy. He could see it in the way that she held herself, the excellent taste she displayed in books, music, and décor. The way she glared at him when she caught his eye, and that smile that he was sure she was unaware she revealed.

Yes, he was attracted to her. Though it would be far too easy to press that point home, Pierre was forced to admit that as his strength gained apace, he found himself wanting to speak with her more.

"Tell me, Helene, how – "

"Helena," she corrected as she bustled past him, taking another shirt from the mending pile and dropping elegantly into a chair – and not, Pierre noticed, the chair beside him.

"Helena," he said quietly, and with such feeling that she started and looked up. Smiling at having gained her attention, Pierre continued, "tell me how your sister and the Duke of...of..."

She smiled, and his stomach twisted as he saw it. "Caershire."

"Yes, that," he said hastily. "How did they meet? How came they to become engaged?"

Her smile faded slightly as she concentrated on the stitching, bringing it closer to her eyes in the fading afternoon sun. "Engaged?"

Pierre nodded, trying to ignore the dexterity of those light fingers.

Helena shrugged, and her smile returned, but it was a shy one. "How does anyone become engaged, I suppose. They met, they liked, they loved."

He watched her cheeks tint a delightful shade of pink, and grinned. She was very conscious of him, that was true – did it stem from an attraction to him, or merely an awareness of his?

"And they are to be married soon?"

She glanced up at him with questioning eyes. "You are very curious. Do you know the Duke?"

Pierre shook his head nonchalantly, and shivered slightly in the cooling evening air. "No, I just wondered. Such different social circles, I thought, it does not seem likely that – "

"You are cold," Helena interrupted, laying aside her mending and reaching for a blanket.

Pierre bristled. "This has gone on long enough, mademoiselle, I am quite well now. A little confusion yesterday, perhaps, but I have fully recovered my strength and I do not need – "

But his voice disappeared the moment that she touched him. Brushing aside his hair from his face in a movement that was intensely intimate, she whispered gently, "I decide when you are well again, Pierre. Now take this."

Her hands now laid a blanket over him, and their fingers touched as he tried to free himself from it.

Their mutual gasp seemed to echo around the empty room. Pierre stared into those sparkling blue eyes which were shimmering with unexpected emotion. Surely she was feeling what he was: the heat of connection, the spark of passion, some sort of connection as if they had always known each other but only just met.

He watched her swallow.

"I will go and find you something to eat," she muttered, and almost fled out of the room.

∾

*H*elena tried to slow her breathing down as she entered the kitchen and leaned against the window.

What had just happened? What was that intensity of emotion that she had never felt before, but had felt so at home in her breast? Why had she been unable to look at Pierre any longer without fire erupting from her stomach and threatening to engulf her body?

Her fingers scraped the window pane, and she breathed out slowly at the coolness of the glass, so different from the quickening pace of her thundering pulse.

At least from here she could not see his handsome face, the prepossessed way that he sat on that sofa, the way his eyes had not left her for more than five minutes that day.

And what eyes. Burning with desire. She did not need to know the intricacies of courtship to see what he wanted from her.

The question was, why did her heart sing out that she wanted it too?

Well, there was nothing to do but pray that her father would return soon. It had been almost three days now, Helena thought looking through the window finally, and not at the glass itself. Surely he would be home soon; it could not be much longer that he would leave her here, alone.

Or worse, not alone.

She sighed, brushed down her hands on the apron she had placed over her gown when she had started the mending, and turned – to find Pierre standing directly behind her.

The shock of having him in such close proximity made her gasp, and her foot slipped. She may not have fallen, but she would never find out as Pierre's hands grabbed hold of her and balanced her.

"Careful, Helena," he said, and the sound of her name finally pronounced correctly caused a little shiver to move up her spine. "You do not want to fall."

I am falling, she wanted to say, but she blushed at the very thought. She barely knew this man, though sickness had certainly revealed a deeper part of his character than one normally saw in an acquaintance of a few days.

And though she was no longer falling, she felt as though her head was still spinning. The strength of his hands, their warmth against her arms, the security of him, the nearness and headiness that it gave her own mind – why, it was enough to –

"No," she said allowed, and with a shake, she dislodged his grip. "No, monsieur, you should be seated, you really must – "

"Oh, *merde*," Pierre said darkly, not moving an inch away from her and affixing her with a determined stare. "You know as well as I do, mademoiselle, that I am quite returned to good health. I have no wish to be set aside like an invalid: I am a man, and I am full of the vigour of life. Put me to good use."

Helena hesitated, and shyly looked at him once more. He certainly looked better; his colour had returned, and there was no sway in his stance as he stood before her.

My, but he was a handsome man.

"Wood," she managed, a simple thought coming to her mind and grasping at it with all she could muster. "There is wood that needs chopping, outside. Wood."

It was all she could do not to hate herself and her folly, but thankfully Pierre did not appear to notice her ability to speak coherently.

"Wood," he repeated, and he smiled a dazzling smile that threatened to overwhelm her. "That I can do, mademoiselle. Just lead the way."

When Helena took a step towards the back door of the little cottage, she was amazed to find that her feet were not made of water after all. It felt impossible, but she was able to move and more with tolerable ease, and within two minutes,

Pierre was chopping wood. Badly, it must be said, Helena smiled to herself, but then she supposed a wealthy noble like Pierre had never come across manual labour in his life.

"And will you watch me, my lady?" Pierre leaned back as he spoke, and grinned at her. "To ensure that the work is done to your precise *caractéristiques*?"

Helena's cheeks burned, and she turned back into the house.

She had intended to take the time to prepare some food for dinner, and yet the moment that she walked past the window and glanced through it, her steps were arrested.

Pierre d'Épiluçon had removed the shirt she had lent him and was throwing the axe over his head, bringing it crashing down onto the wood he had placed before him. Muscles contorted and wrenched with the effort, and beads of sweat had gathered across his forehead, around his shoulders, and down his chest, despite his healing leg.

Helena felt a tug of heat and longing between her legs, and almost gasped aloud at the sight of him. Desire she had read about, heard some of the rougher sailors joke about, but nothing had prepared her for the sweet desperation that she felt when she looked at Pierre in that moment.

It was almost like a hunger: an insatiable thirst, a thirst that would only be quenched by his lips.

"Enjoying the view?"

Helena's cheeks went scarlet. Lost in her own thoughts, Pierre had paused his work, and was mopping his brow with the back of his hand as he chuckled at her.

"I..." Helena started instinctively, but had no comprehension of what words were supposed to come next. "I..."

"Well, if you are then I am afraid to tell you, mademoiselle, that the wood is all quite chopped, and your entertainment is at an end," said the striking gentleman who had collapsed outside her house and was now sparking feelings in her that had to be repressed. "If you will permit me, I will return to my sofa."

Helena had hoped that her ability to speak would have returned by the time he had re-entered the house, but he decided to do so whilst carrying the shirt, rather than wearing it, and she found herself so utterly transfixed that it was several minutes later, and thankfully when his shirt had been returned to its rightful place, that she was able to enter the parlour once more.

"I must admit to feeling a little restless," he was saying as she walked in. "Back to full health, as I am. I must compliment you on your nursing."

Helena smiled weakly, and dropped into the chair furthest away from him. She couldn't be too careful. "I wanted to get you back to fighting fit, and I am pleased that I have been able to do so."

Pierre returned her smile, but there was far more heat in it. "Ah, Helena. Your touch is revitalising more than you could possibly know."

There was that blush again: there was nothing she could do to stop it, and still it would come!

"My father will be pleased to make your acquaintance, when he returns," she managed, twisting her fingers in her lap to remind herself that she needed to keep talking. "He has gone to Marshurst, the nearest market town, for...for a few days."

"And will he be back this evening?"

Helena started, and glared up at him, but nothing but innocence suffused across Pierre's face – if you could call it innocence. There was a sparkle of some mischief in his eye that was incredibly becoming, lighting up his face and dazzling it, illuminating the handsomeness that it already possessed.

As if it needed improving.

"Sadly not," Helena finally said. "Which means that the same bed – the sofa here – is still available for you tonight, should you wish it."

Pierre's smile broadened. "I would rather have yours."

She had not thought it possible for her cheeks to burn any deeper, but it was. For a moment, the image of Pierre d'Épiluçon lying beside her in her bed, flashed across her mind – but the imagined Pierre did not stay still for long. He was moving closer to her, closer than he had ever been, and though she knew she should move away from him, there did not seem to be any point: she wanted to be close to him, she wanted to feel his lips on hers, she –

She started, and jerked out of the vision. Pierre was looking at her curiously, and if she was not mistaken, he had a rather too clear idea of what was just running through her mind.

"Rest yourself easy, mademoiselle," he said quietly. "I would never make you do something that you are uncomfortable with. Having said that...the offer is there."

Helena tried to swallow, but her throat seemed to have been dried out like a mackerel. "I...I would recommend separate beds, monsieur."

Pierre threw up his hands in that French way of his that she was starting to find endearing, and rose. "So be it, mademoiselle Helena. Lead the way."

For the first time in her life, Helena was heartily conscious of a man's gaze on her body. She found his eyes staring at her as she moved around the room, trimming the lamps and candles. He could not stop watching her, it seemed, as they stepped up the narrow staircase – and when they reached the tiny landing where the two bedrooms led from, he paused, and those eyes raked over her body once again.

"This is goodnight, then," he said in a low voice, his eyes transfixed on hers.

Helena nodded, rather than trusting her own voice.

In a swift movement, Pierre took her right hand and brought it to his lips, kissing it lightly and honourably. "I have never felt this indebted," he murmured, "nor more happily indebted to another person. Thank you. For saving my life."

She could feel the heat of his hand on hers, and the spot where his lips had brushed it, but now there was a gentle tug on that hand and she had taken a step towards him.

Pierre was close, very close, too close, and yet Helena felt deep in her heart that he was not close enough – and now he was leaning, tilting ever so gently, giving her plenty of time to lean away if that was her desire.

But it was not. She wanted him, wanted to allow him to do what he was about to do, and her eyelashes fluttered shut as his lips touched hers.

The kiss was light at first; like a butterfly landing on a flower, unwilling to disturb its natural peace. And then it deepened: Pierre had dropped her hand but his own were now around her waist, and he was kissing her, kissing her like his life depended on it, kissing her like she was air and he a drowning man. Her lips had parted to allow him in, and he was tendering kissing her and her whole body now seemed to be alive, and her hands were resting on his chest and she could feel his heart beating quickly and it was matching the beat of her own.

"Oh, Helena," he murmured for a moment, breaking the

connection, but she raised her lips to his once more and kissed him, for the first time.

He had not been expected it, but his passionate return of her exploratory kiss was enough to tell her that it was wanted. He moaned slightly in her mouth, and it made her clutch him all the more, and then one of his hands moved down from her waist and cupped her bottom.

Helena broke away from him and stepped back, breathing heavily.

She looked with lust dripping eyes at Pierre, who was panting.

"G-Good night," she managed, before she escaped to the sanctuary of her own room, and lay on the bed, fully clothed, heart pounding, and body aching.

6

---

*I*t was no use. Hiding up here was ridiculous, Helena told herself, and eventually she simply would have to go downstairs.

The little clock that had been her mother's chimed beside her bed. It was ten o'clock. There was no putting it off any longer.

"*Bonjour,*" was the word accompanied with the beaming smile of Pierre d'Épiluçon as she stepped into the parlour. "And what a beautiful day it is too!"

Helena blinked. It was as though a newly instructed butler had whirled through the room in an attempt to impress his new master...but had not done a particularly good job of it. The blanket had been badly folded and placed underneath the sofa, which had been brushed down but with a mop, by the look of it. There were wet streaks across the cotton.

The floor was spotless, but there was a vase missing, and if the sharps of fractured glass were any indication, it had been broken. However, someone had been resourceful with the flowers that had been picked from her garden, and placed them in a new jug. Which was a saucepan.

The entire room gave a picture of a person, and Helena could not help but smile as she thought of who, desperate to make a good impression but with no idea of how do to it.

"*Voila!*" Pierre was standing by the kitchen door, erect, tall, and proud. "You like? I am not sure what your favourite flowers are, mademoiselle, but as there were so many roses in your garden, I thought – "

"Yes," she murmured, stepping into the room and smiling at the pile of mending that had been shoved behind the sofa to hide it – not, presumably, part of the décor. "Thank you."

He watched her as she examined the room, and she did not need to see him to know that he was two things: perfectly healthy, and undressing her with his gaze.

"And now all that remains is to see my boat," Pierre was saying. "Will you accompany me, mademoiselle Helena? I must see how damaged it is."

"I warn you," she said quietly, picking up her shawl to wrap around her shoulders and around the collar of her gown. "It is unlikely to ever be seaworthy again."

He shrugged, and something in her stomach twisted to see that nonchalant movement. "It is, it is not, we will see."

They were greeted, as they stepped outside, with a warm breeze, warmer than Helena would have expected this springtime. It ruffled her hair, but it did not cool her.

"'Tis a strange, changeable weather we are having," she murmured.

"Here, let me take," Pierre began, reaching out for her hand.

But Helena was too quick for him; slipping deftly to the side, in complete control, she laughed at his surprise.

"I have spent many a year walking on these stones," she smiled, watching the Frenchman struggle with his footing. "'Tis no surprise that I have got the better of it than you."

That she was better – more nimble, almost spritely – was impossible to deny. Helena giggled as Pierre slipped and slid over the wet stones of the beach, wincing at the tug in his healing leg, and though he did not see the joke at first, he could not help but laugh at the delicate way that she walked, while he crashed alongside her.

"I will admit, I am impressed," he said, throwing her a smile. "Your athleticism, it is most impressive."

For a moment, she thought he was laughing at her; but as she turned her head, and gazed at him, she saw nothing but sincerity.

"Well, it is what I do," she said, smiling back at him. "I tend to and heal the sailors and fisherman that get thrown back onto shore, and sometimes that makes them very difficult to reach. You have to be nimble, and not mind the sharpness of some of the stones."

She felt, rather than saw his gaze drop down.

"You are not wearing any shoes!"

Helena laughed. "You feel the movement of the stones, their strength or slipperiness, far better without shoes. I have grown accustomed to walking barefoot on my beach."

"Oh, 'tis your beach, is it?"

They laughed together, and Helena felt joy surge through her. This – whatever this was – was wonderful. He was always making her laugh, putting a smile on her face. If only he could make her laugh for the rest of her –

Helena shook herself. She should not think like that.

"So you are a rescuer," Pierre said softly as his ship-wrecked boat came into view. "And I can tell you, mademoiselle Helena, that no matter what choppy waters you have found in my soul, you have certainly rescued me."

She coloured, and was silent, but the warmth that was stirring up in her was starting to make her heart ache. She wanted him to kiss her; to kiss her like he had done at the top of the stairs just hours before.

Did she have the bravery – or perhaps, the stupidity to kiss him?

"Ah, it looks much worse than I had thought." Pierre's voice interrupted her thoughts as his despondency showed.

Helena took a close look, and had to agree. "Without your mast, you cannot sail in her again – I am surprised that you were able to come this far. Your stern has buckled, that will need a repair, and," ducking around him to check the rear of the boat, "yes, 'tis as I thought. Your rudder is heavily damaged, that will need to be replaced, not repaired."

She stood up again, and smiled at the astonished look on Pierre's handsome face.

"You...you know so much," he said, shaking his head. "I will have to learn not to underestimate you in future."

Future? Helena wanted to ask, but could not bring herself to. Does that mean you will stay here? Stay with me?

Instead, she said, "The damage is not too severe inside, though there is little of it, I suppose, to even be damaged."

Though it was tilted slightly to one side, it only took a hefty push from Helena to right it, nestled as it was by the sand and stones on each side. She stepped into it, and turned to smile at Pierre.

"We will have you shipshape in no time."

But Pierre was not smiling. He was looking at her with such seriousness, such a fierceness, that she gasped.

"I would happily live every day with you," he said in a

low voice, heavy with emotion, "if it meant I could see you smile like that each of those days."

Helena's heart swelled: so captivated by his words, and his meaning – he wanted to stay with her, he was going to stay – that her foot slipped on the hull of the boat.

Strong arms caught her, and she gasped at the intensity of his hold. She nestled into that strength, her footing found but her heart cast off and lost in the swirling gale of emotions.

The desire to kiss him was starting to overwhelm her, and she stared up into Pierre's eyes that were staring down at her with equally matched passion.

"I will not," he whispered in a heavy tone, "do anything that you do not want me to do, *Helene*."

Helena smiled, pushed up on her toes, and kissed him full on the mouth.

And she almost cried out against his lips at the hot sensations that ran through her body as she made contact with him, so immediate was the response to his touch. Perhaps it was because he kissed her back with even more ardour; perhaps it was because she was barely aware of where she was standing, how she was standing, if she was standing.

The arms that had just recently been holding her upright were now tightening their grip on her, as though she was the only anchor in a storm, and Pierre's lips were forceful on hers but with passion.

Helena opened her lips and allowed him entrance into her mouth, and almost cried out again as his tongue gently caressed her own. Her hands were clutching his chest and she could feel his hastily beating heart through the thin shirt he was wearing.

"Oh, *Helene*," Pierre murmured in a dark voice as he

broke away from her, staring at her with such fiery eyes that
something deep within her melted.

"Pierre," she gasped, breathless, heart racing, giddy with
lust, ready to give her all to him but unsure what that even
meant. "I-I want – Pierre, I want – "

"I know," he said with a smile, and it was filled with such
passion that Helena felt a warmth creep between her legs.
"Come here."

The remains of the sail were pooled at the bottom of the
little boat, and in one swift movement Pierre removed his
shirt and laid it down as a pillow.

Helena barely noticed what he was doing: the sight of his
bare chest made her breasts ache, and she wanted to touch
him, for him to touch her, to caress her, to kiss her – she had
never felt this wanton, never wanted a man like this in her life.

"Lie here," Pierre said jaggedly, as though struggling for
breath.

Helena obeyed, lying on the sail with her head resting
on his shirt. It smelt of his musky smell, and the ache in her
stomach clenched tighter.

"I want you," she said simply, reaching out for him, lips
aquiver and eyes pooled with desire.

If she had expected him to try and resist her, she was
wrong. Uttering a low groan and her name, Pierre
descended to her, covering her body with his own, kissing
her frantically as his hurried hands clutched at her hips.
She did gasp in his mouth this time as the heat building
between her legs caused her unconsciously to spread them,
allowing him closer to her as he became entangled with her.

There seemed to be too many clothes in the way, Helena
thought wildly as he began to kiss her neck, and there was a
tug at the ribbon at the front of her gown, and it was open,

and her breasts, swollen with lust and the fever of love, fell out.

There was no time for shame or embarrassment: the moment that she was aware of being exposed, Pierre dipped his head and took a nipple in his mouth.

Her whole body convulsed at the pleasure that shot through her body and she whimpered, "Pierre!"

This only seemed to drive on onwards, as his hand reached her other breast and caressed it, as his left hand remained on her hip, squeezing it, lifting it up so that the hardness she could feel between her legs rubbed against her.

Pierre groaned into her, and releasing her nipple poured an ocean of kisses onto her mouth, light at first, and then deeper and deeper until Helena thought she would lose herself in him, and she was glad, because this joy and heat rising in her had to go somewhere.

Her hands, nervously at first, now explored his chest, his hand, and when she accidently scratched him in her own passion, Pierre cried out in barely controlled ecstasy.

"God, *Helene,* what are you doing to me?" He muttered darkly, smiling down at her as he took a moment from worshipping her lips.

"Pierre," she moaned, the heat building in her. "I need you – I want you, I want – "

He stopped her mouth with his own, but his hands left her and struggled with his britches, and in a short moment Helena gasped to see the nakedness of the man she now knew she loved, beyond a shadow of a doubt.

Those quick fingers grabbed at her shirt, pushing them up as her breasts moved in the hurried movement. The sight of them seemed to transfix Pierre, and for a moment Helena glorified in her power. To think that her body should have such an effect on a man like Pierre.

He growled and lowered his head to nuzzle, kiss, and play with her breasts once more, and in the sheer pleasure that he was giving her, Helena arched her back and cried out his name.

The sound of his name made Pierre jerk up, but he did nothing but kiss her once more, raise her skirts, and plunge himself into her.

Helena did not know what was happening until it had happened, and then there was such sweet intimacy between them that she hardly knew what to do with herself. Squirming slightly at the odd sensation, she saw Pierre jerk at the feeling, and smiled as she gently moved her hips in a circle.

"Oh, *Helene, mon dieu,* what are you – "

But Pierre hardly seemed able to speak, and Helena, losing her hesitancy in the giddiness of her power over him, moved her hands to tenderly caress, and then bitingly clutch at his buttocks as her hips moved in a rhythmic circle.

Leaning on his elbows, Pierre seemed barely able to control his own breathing, let alone speak, and Helena tipped her lips upwards to capture his own and tasted the heady heat on his tongue.

"I want more," she moaned into his neck as he seemed unable to move. "Give me more, Pierre."

That there was more, she was in no doubt; the rising heat, the tugging sensation of him inside her: it was all leading to something, though she knew not what. Her desperate words, however, seemed to spark him to life.

With a devilish grin, Pierre pulled back her hands from his body and pinned them above her head against the rough sail. She struggled against him for a moment, and she saw his eyes flutter at the sensation of her straining against him, and she arched her back to try and feel him deeper.

"More," she cried, and catching his eye and tightening her legs around him, she moaned, "I am begging you, Pierre!"

That was it. With a shout of desperate longing, Pierre dipped his head to hers whilst keeping her arms pinned to the bottom of the boat, and began thrusting into her slowly, never quite leaving her, and never quite filling her.

"Yes, yes," Helena cried, unable to stop herself. "Faster!"

"Slower," came Pierre's jerking voice, straining for control. "Trust me, Helena, trust me!"

It was impossible not to cry out with the pleasure of it, and he joined her groans with grunts of his own, interspersed with her name as he slowly increased the speed and depth at which he sunk that most private part of himself into the warm sticky heat of her body.

"Helena," he cried, and as though unable to ignore her trembling breasts any longer, he attacked one with kisses and then the other.

Helena thought that she would collapse with the sensations that were pouring through her body, and as her back tried to arch again but couldn't with the weight of his passionate rhythm, she felt the heat boil up in her to a peak that she thought she could not endure.

"Pierre!" She screamed out as the ecstasy overwhelmed her, and he was shudderingly pounding into her and crying out her own name.

"Helena – my only, my one, my sweetest Helena!" As he poured himself into her, he poured out sweet nothings into her ear as her body shook with the waves of joy that washed over her, and then he collapsed across her, and nuzzled her neck.

⌒

*I*t was the sun now caressing his face, but Pierre felt so happy he was almost drunk. The sunlight warmed his naked body, and under his arm, another naked body rested peacefully beside him.

Helena. What a woman. As the seagulls cried out mournfully overhead, there was nothing but joy in his heart, and pleasant fatigue in his limbs.

"What amazes me," he whispered, raising his hand to stroke her hair, "is that no one heard us."

A gentle chuckle vibrated against his chest. "Yes," she agreed jestingly, "and you were hardly quiet!"

Pierre gasped in mock outrage, and brought his fingers down to tickle the sun warmed body nestled close to him, and she giggled. He kissed the top of her head, and prayed that this moment would never end.

"You know," Helena murmured finally, "there is no one living for a mile around. I have told you that. This is essentially our own private beach."

Pierre's heart swelled. This was, after all, his own portion of paradise. Though a hellish storm had brought him here, it was to a true heaven.

"Perhaps you are the rich one after all," he murmured with a smile, and raised her head to kiss his beloved full on the mouth.

7

*I*t had taken them almost three hours to drag themselves away from the boat on the beach: the chance to explore each other's bodies, completely alone with nature, was too great. But eventually, hunger of the stomach overrode hunger of the heart, and they dressed, and made their way back to the cottage.

"And I really must have my own things again," Pierre chuckled as he opened the front door for Helena to walk through. "It does seem strange, wearing someone else's clothes. Where are mine?"

Helena pointed to her pile of mending. "I washed and dried them as best I could, but they are sorely torn, so I wanted to – "

He threw himself onto the sofa, no longer a prison so able to be enjoyed, and grinned. "You do far too much for me, *mon ange*. I do not deserve you."

For a moment, he thought she was going to disagree with him, and then she laughed. "Perhaps you are right!"

Still laughing, she wandered through into the kitchen muttering something about tea, and Pierre smiled as he watched her go. What an incredible woman: to give herself to him so freely, to relish the chance to share such joy with him – and not to shy away from him now, now that he had seen all and touched all...

He shifted uncomfortably. If he was not careful, he would find himself growing hard again for her, and even he could not expect her to allow him that freedom here, in her home.

Moving across to one end of the sofa, Pierre picked up his jacket from the mending pile and smiled. All traces of his horrendous sea journey had been expunged; you would hardly know that it had even been wet, let alone doused in seawater.

His smile faded as he recalled the moment that his mother had given him the jacket, and he shook his head, as though to shake the memory away from him. There was no use dwelling on such things, no point at all.

Pierre moved the jacket to reach into the pockets, and found...nothing.

He fought the disappointment as he reminded himself that he was lucky to be alive, let alone with the jacket still after that riot in Whiteridge. But to have come so far with his mother and sister's jewels, and to lose them in the depths of the Channel...

Throwing the jacket down in disgust, Pierre watched a button break off its meagre thread, and roll under the sofa. He sighed, reached down, and drew out not just the button, but a small wooden box.

It was curiously hidden, and Pierre's curiosity was not something he had ever learned to control. He pulled the box out, placed it on his knee, and opened it.

His mouth fell open. Lying on top of what looked like a series of letters were his family jewels.

A quick scrabble was enough to tell him that they were all there. It was unaccountable: how had they been rescued from the depths of the sea to rest in this small box.

"The tea will be ready shortly!" Helena's voice called out from the kitchen.

Pierre slowly raised his head. Helena. She was the only one who could have done it: gone through his pockets when she was about to wash the jacket, and realised that he would not want such jewels to be mangled.

But then, why place them in this box?

Pierre looked around the room. There were few other places, it was true, where such jewellery could be placed in safety. That must be it, he told himself. They had been placed here for safekeeping. What other explanation could there be?

But his heart sank as he looked around the room more carefully: the fading wallpaper, torn in some places. The frequently scrubbed but never truly clean floor, the mending pile that never ended.

It would be very tempting to take these jewels and trade them for a better life.

As soon as the thought had entered his head, he felt ashamed of himself. Did he really think that little of Helena? Had she given him any reason to think that she was a thief?

No. Everything she did was from elegance and kindness, and he would be a brute to suspect anything ill of her.

Pierre bit his lip, and wished to God that he had not found the box which he soon placed back underneath the sofa.

〜

a nd yet with the box out of sight, it could not be put out of Pierre's mind. That evening he could feel the coldness in his voice and he tried to pour the affection that he felt for Helena over it, masking the suspicion.

"You are very quiet," she said with a look that he could not understand.

She was seated on the sofa, curled up at one end while he sat at the other.

He shrugged. "Perhaps."

"I do not think that there is any perhaps about it," Helena continued, nudging him with her foot with a smile. "Is anything amiss?"

Pierre did not know what to say. 'Did you try and steal my family's inheritance' was quite a bold statement to make, and not one that he felt he could do with any justice. The closeness that he had felt, that utter nakedness that he had experienced with her, seemed gone, and it was his own doing. She still looked at him with the eyes of a lover.

"I am afraid the little food available to me is a little repetitive," she said quietly, gazing into his face as though attempting to read his mind. "Does it fatigue you, to have the same meal over and over again?"

Wild horses would not drag the truth from him, which was a very certain yes; Pierre knew too much of her relative poverty now to make such an assertion.

"Not at all," he assured her, with what he hoped was a winning smile. But he drifted back into silence once more as the thought of his possessions, hidden in a small wooden box out of his sight, returned to his mind.

She looked at him, curiously. Her hair was unpinned, flowing down her shoulders and back, ever-present earrings dangling down, and her face was so open and vulnerable that Pierre could not help but smile, albeit gently. Helena was not a woman to do such a thing, surely.

But what if he was wrong? The temptation, he knew, would be very great – and while he could not imagine living like this, in these circumstances, for long, he had experienced enough of hunger during his time on that godforsaken boat: enough fear of safety, longing for water, and hope of warm shelter, to know that he would probably have robbed anyone who had come in his path to attain such securities.

"You are a thousand miles away," Helena cut into his thoughts as she poked him with her foot again. "France?"

Pierre forced a smile, and lied. "Yes. I know that it is not so far away, but it feels a great distance now that I know the boat is essentially irreparable."

"Oh, I would not say so," she said warmly, but with a smile that appeared sad rather than joyful. "A little coin will be required, of course, to get it back on an even keel, but I suppose that will not be...you have said before how wealthy you are, so..."

That was the moment, Pierre often said when he looked back at that evening, that he should have asked her. It was a natural statement, to explain that he had lost his jewels, his fortune, in the ocean during the crossing: he could then wait and see whether she revealed that she had kept them for safekeeping – or hide the fact that she had stolen them for her own use.

But it was not to be. Just as he opened his mouth, half desperately hoping that something would occur to interrupt them for he knew not how to approach such a delicate matter, there was a knock at the door.

Helena jumped up, startled. "Hide!"

Pierre stared at his hissing host. "Hide?"

She gestured at him to ascend the stairs and nodded. "Do you think my reputation will be able to withstand the discovery of a strange man – and a Frenchman, to boot! – in my home, without my father there?"

She spoke in a low hurried tone, but Pierre quickly understood her. Rising from the sofa he threw himself across the room, and only managed to climb up to the fourth step when the door was opened.

"My, Mrs Thatcher," he heard Helena say warmly. "What brings you out here on such a brisk and cold night? I am not needed, am I?"

The anxious tone that she ended her statement on was not lost on Pierre, who scowled. It was difficult tô remember, sometimes, that Helena also rescued others from the depths of that beast of an ocean – and yet how could he claim her all to himself, when he had known her only but a few days?

The memory of her naked body, covered in the sun's rays, sprang to his memory, and he grinned. Ah, he would always be her possessor in his heart.

"...strange direction," he caught from an older woman's voice. "But then I could not think where else to go."

"'Tis a strange direction indeed," Helena's voice agreed as Pierre stood still on the stairs. "But I think I comprehend its import. My father spent some time in France, oh, above ten years ago. This letter must be from one of his business acquaintance – I will keep it, thank you Mrs Thatcher, and return it to you if I am in error. Good evening."

By the sound of it, she did not give Mrs Thatcher the chance to disagree with her decision; the door was shut, and a whispered voice encouraged Pierre to descend once more.

When he entered the parlour, Helena was holding a letter out to him.

"'To the Frenchman'," she quoted with a smile, indicating the letter. "I can have no doubt as to its intended recipient, though goodness knows why Mrs Thatcher thought to enquire here – "

"Or how anyone knows that I am here," Pierre said with a frown, taking the letter and inspecting the handwriting. "I did not think anyone was aware of my escape from France. Someone must be...watching the house."

They both stared at the letter in his hand.

"Well," sighed Helena eventually. "You will never know unless you open it."

Pierre stared down at the letter. It was written on paper quite elegant and smooth, richly bought, and the writing was elegant and formal. If he did not know any better...

He sat on the sofa, turned over the letter, and his heart jumped.

No. It could not be. It simply was not possible.

His own seal stared back at him: the rampant lion emblazoned on an E.

Heart now thundering, his fingers tore at the seal and opened up the letter to read the fine handwriting evenly laid across the paper in lines.

My darling Pierre,

If you are reading this letter, God be praised! It has reached you at last, and its constant wanderings over this sad globe have been at least as long as our own.

My brother, it has been with the greatest secrecy that I have been living this past year, and I am sure that you will forgive the privacy that has removed even yourself from my intimacy and insight, but it was a necessary precaution.

You were being watched, dear Pierre, in France. If you are still there, in our own country, then I beg that you would leave it as soon as you complete this letter. If you have already

escaped, then I recommend caution. I have given this to my
trusted network, and if it reaches you, then Paendly should not
be too far behind.

Trust no one. Believe nothing. Make no friends save those
you need to survive. The tendrils of the Revolution are not
confined to the borders of our once great country; they spread
far and wide.

I cannot reveal my location as yet, but I hope to see you
before too long. I will know where to find you. Do not attempt
to discover me, no matter the temptation, for you would put us
both at risk.

Until I see you again, little brother, I remain your
affectionate and loyal sister,

Giselle

Pierre hurriedly drew breath, his lungs aching as he
realised they had been absolutely still while he had been
reading Giselle's letter.

Oh, to see her handwriting once more! To know that she
was alive, that she was surviving somewhere out there in the
world, perhaps not too far away! He scanned the lines again:
it would be sensible, indeed, if she had urged him to leave
France immediately, to assume that she had already
done so.

His heart leapt. She could be here, in England: there was
every chance that he could see her again!

"Does it bring good news?"

The casual question broke into his thoughts and
stunned him, bringing him crashing down to reality: a small
poor house on the edge of the coast of England.

"Yes," he managed to say with relative calm. "Yes, I think
it is good news."

But as he spoke, he stared at the handwriting. Could he

be sure that it was Giselle? Could it be a trick, a trap perhaps? But then, and he read the final paragraph hastily once more, she does not ask his own whereabouts, and is coy with her own. If it were to be a trap, then surely his location would be sought?

Helena lowered herself to sit beside him on the sofa. "Is it from Giselle?"

Pierre glanced up hurriedly, and hid the letter from her view. "Giselle? Why do you suppose that?"

Her eyes widened at the sharpness of his tone, but he could not help it. How could she know – did she send it, perhaps? Was this all a conspiracy to –

"You said that she was your only surviving family member," Helena said softly, with a frown. "Who else could the letter be from?"

Pierre relaxed, but kept the letter hidden. Well, that certainly made sense, he could not fault her logic.

"What does she say?"

Was he becoming paranoid now? The jewellery, hidden; the letter, so easily coming to him when no one else in the world knew that he was here?

Pierre smiled, and tucked the letter away. "Nothing of import."

8

*H*elena awoke the next morning with joy in her heart and excitement in her lungs.

Well. So it was not only her sister who was to be married: here she had her own shipwrecked suitor, almost deposited in her very lap by the ocean, to have and to hold, for richer for poorer – and here she had to laugh, alone as she was in her bedroom.

He had been rich, and now he was poor, and she loved him – yes, she could admit to herself that she loved him – no matter the size of his purse.

After such an incredible day yesterday, baring her very soul to him, baring her body and allowing such sweet pleasures to overwhelm them both, Helena laid back in bed and thought of the life that they were to have together.

Not here; she did not want to stay any longer. Perhaps in a cottage, on the Duke of Caershire's estate. They could dine every evening together, and surely the Duke and Pierre would have much to speak of. They were not so different, in their own ways.

Helena smiled. As long as none of the Duke's family had

fought France in the recent wars, they should be safe from politics!

A gentle stirring noise could be heard through the wall. He was awake. His strange gentlemanly standards had forbidden him from joining her in her bed last night, and she had to admit that he had looked a little strange. But then, the letter.

As the memories of the evening before seeped into her consciousness, Helena frowned. The letter, tidings which she had assumed would revive his strangely low spirits, had done nothing but to increase them. He had gone to bed early so low that her kiss and caress had been brushed aside, and she had felt piqued until the thought of such a letter from her own sister would have undoubtedly cast her own spirits down.

But now, and Helena smiled and rose from her bed, it was a new day. A day in which they could start planning their live together – a day of joy, and merriment, and excitement!

When would they marry? Helena wondered as she silently dressed. Not too close to her sister, she hoped, otherwise there would be a mighty fine confusion. Perhaps in two months; that would give the Duke and Duchess – and she could not but laugh as she traipsed down the stairs at the thought of her sister, a duchess! – time for their honeymoon.

"Oh!" She cried as she entered the parlour. She had thought herself quite alone in being awake so early, and yet there he was. "Good morning, Pierre!"

She crossed the room lightly, and kissed him full on the mouth – and found to her joy that he reciprocated with a strength of ardour that almost took her breath away.

When they broke apart, they were both panting slightly

out of breath, and Pierre was smiling. "Now that is a wonderful way to greet the morning."

Helena laughed. "Well, you may as well get used to it!"

Bustling through to the kitchen to start the tea, she heard Pierre say, "Ah, it will be a painful thing to leave you, my dear Helena."

At first, the words did not entirely register in her mind: so concerned was she with fetching some water, considering what victuals she would need to purchase that day – and if only Mrs Montgomery could be persuaded to exchange some of her mending for eggs, they would have a very pretty meal – that the meaning of Pierre's words did not sink in.

"Leave?" She called through vaguely. "When will you be back?"

Footsteps told her that Pierre had moved through to the kitchen, but she did not turn to face him until he said, "Back?"

Helena stared at him, and blinked. "Yes, back. It would be much easier for me to ascertain what to tell my father, and exactly how much food to buy, and those sorts of things, if I knew how long you were to be gone for."

It was only then that she noticed a strange sadness in the smile that broke across his face, and it caused her heart to twinge.

"Helena," Pierre said gently, taking her hands in his. "I am most grateful for the kind attentions that you have bestowed on me, I truly am, and I will happily admit that I probably would have perished, out there on that beach, or here in the depths of my fever, if you had not been my rescuer – "

A sense of foreboding crept across her heart, and Helena started to understand his meaning. "Pierre, you cannot mean – surely you are not trying to tell me that – "

" – but as for staying here," Pierre said gently with a low laugh. "You must see that it is impossible. I need to find my sister – ascertain, I suppose, whether she is truly alive – and then we, my sister and I, will try to see what sort of life we can build for ourselves."

"I will come with you," Helena said immediately, feeling the warmth in his hands and not understanding why he wanted to undertake such a journey alone. "After all, why should a man travel without his wife?"

There was a moment of stillness in the air that hung between them for well over a minute. Helena did not wish to break it, so delicate it seemed to be, and Pierre just stood before her, open mouthed, her hands still in his.

Finally, he broke the silence by saying in a choked voice, "Wife?"

She broke free of his grip, and gathered her hands together nervously. "Of course. I know that we cannot be married overly soon, it will take time – and to be frank, I would much love to have your sister there, so we will need to find her first before we – "

"Wife," Pierre repeated, interrupting her. Helena saw that his cheeks were pale, and his brows furrowed. "Wife."

~

*P*ierre gazed at her, horrified.

Helena was nodding, but less certainly than she had but minutes before. "Why, of course."

"But Helena – I have made you no promises," he said hoarsely. "Indeed, I have been in great care to ensure that I do not!"

The horror in his own heart was now matched on the beautiful face before him. "Great care to ensure? Why,

Pierre, you have given such assurances of your affection that I have been slightly overwhelmed by it! How can you tell me that you have made no promises?"

Pierre took a few steps back, and then turned to walk into the parlour. He wracked his brains hurriedly: had he made any such declaration? Had the word love ever passed his lips?

"It was not so formally done," said Helena quietly, just behind him. "And yet surely no one could have believed any differently from the way that we have been together. Why, Pierre, when we made love in your boat – "

"I said nothing of marriage!" Pierre interrupted, though the vision of Helena in a pale blue dress at the altar of his family church now flashed before his mind, and it pained him to think how right it was. No, he had nothing to offer her, he could not possibly offer such a union!

"I gave you myself!" Helena's voice was slightly raised now, still gentle, but firm, with a grip of iron on her emotions, it was clear to see. "Do you think that I offer such intimacy to everyone that I rescue?"

Pierre laughed at the very thought of his good Helena doing such a thing, but it did not calm her feelings.

"Do not laugh at me!" She stepped forward with such intention that Pierre quickly took a step back. "The intimacy that we have shared has been enough of a statement, Pierre d'Épiluçon. Do you think I would have allowed you to make love to me if I had not thought marriage was truly in your heart?"

Her voice broke at the end of her statement, and a little part of Pierre's heart broke too. Had he really been so callous as to think that Helena would be strong enough, or cold enough, as he was? To enjoy the pleasures of the flesh without expecting anything in return?

"Helena – my only, my one, my sweetest Helena."

That was what he had said to her – and in that moment of passion and adoration of her body, he had meant it!

Only now could he see the way that Helena could have heard those words, and heard wedding bells.

"I...I have made no promises," he repeated, as though it were a piece of flotsam on the ocean that he was clinging to for dear life. "Helena, you must understand that I have intense affection for you, but to offer you marriage...it is not in my power to do so."

There was real pain on her features now, genuine and heart-breaking. He was breaking her heart, and Pierre hated himself for it – but what had he to offer her? A life on the road, in hiding, in desperate looking for a woman that may no longer live?

"I see," she said, dropping into a chair with such dull tones that bile rose in his throat. "I see now. I was just a distraction. A way to waste time until you heard from your sister. A chance for you to take your pleasure. Fortunate for you that I have no one to protect me, to fight for my honour here – for if I had a brother, he would surely challenge you, *monsieur,* to do what is right! And perhaps when my sister is married, Alexander will do just that!"

A flicker of anger sparked in his soul now as Pierre glared at the woman who both infuriated him and soothed him. "Ah, happy for you that you have such connections!" The bitterness was impossible to remove from his voice, and he hated himself as he saw Helena flinch. "You have a sister living, safe and sound, protected and unafraid of the world around her. Would that I could claim such joy too!"

"Why cannot you see that you can have both – you do not have to choose between us! 'Tis not your sister before you, but a woman who loves you!" Helena cried out with tears in her eyes, almost as though she could not stop herself. "Why not think of her, for a moment? We could find Giselle together!"

"'Tis too dangerous! And how can I even trust you – where is this father that you keep talking about? Why have my jewels been taken from my possession, why have you been going through my possessions?"

"My father is a drunk!" Helena shot back at him, her cheeks pink. "You think I would not like to know where he is? 'Tis no fault of mine if he disappears for weeks at a time, and as for your jewels – "

"Yes, you thief!" Pierre shot back at her, hating his own words but seeming unable to stop himself.

"Do you love me?" Helena asked him urgently. "For I love you – more ardently than I can ever express."

Pierre's heart stopped. She loved him. Of course she did, he had been in no doubt of that since the moment that she had kissed him in the boat. He had known it, and the real question was, why was he hiding his own feelings from her – from himself?

"Do you love me?" She repeated with eyes pouring out hope. "If you love me, Pierre, please tell me. Do not lose the opportunity to love because you are eager to find another you care about."

Pierre opened his mouth to say he knew not what, just knowing that he had to tell her, he could not leave her without assuring her of his affections – when they were interrupted by a loud knock at the door.

"Pierre?" A man's voice called out, strong and concerned. "*Êtes-vous là*, Pierre? Open this door!"

Pierre stared at Helena, and watched her dash away the tears from her eyes.

"It is for you," she said dully. "Perhaps it is Giselle.

Perhaps it is someone who can take you away from here. That is what you what, is not it?"

He wanted to retort that he hated the thought of ever leaving her, but he must be true to his sister who needed him, but another loud knock interrupted his thoughts, and he strode over to the front door and flung it open.

"It is you – thank God, for I have no wish to travel about hunting for a shipwrecked Frenchman the rest of my life!"

Pierre blinked in the blinding sunlight, and then saw the shape of James appear before him. "James?"

His old childhood friend guffawed with laughter. "Goodness, you have certainly taken a beating if you are struggling to recognise me – though I cannot say I blame you, for you have certainly been roughing it if I am any judge. I heard the news from...well, we can discuss that later."

James, the Viscount Paendly, had been a part of Pierre's landscape his entire life; their mothers had been childhood friends. Never before had he been so irritated to see him, and watch him peer into the house where, for but a few days, he had been so happy.

"My word, what an adventure you have been having!" James strode past Pierre into the room, and gave the woman that he loved a cursory glance. "Did you bring a servant with you, Pierre, or did you pick this one up as you went?"

For the first time in his life, Pierre realised exactly how he must seem to others: watching James' well-meaning but rude conduct, seeing how he treated Helena not as though it were her home, but her station to serve him as he thrust his travelling cloak in her arms – he must have been reprehensible.

No wonder Helena had been sharp with him when he had first arrived here; and yet, Pierre thought with an aching heart, how much he had changed thanks to her good offices, her sweet temper.

"I do not think we shall stay long," said James, poking his head in the kitchen and curling up his nose. "'Tis a long way back to Paendly, and I would rather be on the road before eleven, if it is all the same to you, d'Épiluçon. You have little luggage, I presume?"

Pierre forced a laugh. "Almost none, I would say."

"Here," came a gentle voice, and Pierre started to see Helena holding out his own clothes, freshly washed, dried, and mended, with a small wooden box that he recognised lying on top. "Your belongings, sir."

The last word was forcibly servile, and he wanted to tell her that there was no need to speak to him like that; that he had nothing but strong emotion for her – but could he say love? Not with Paendly standing there like an idiot.

"By Jove, d'Épiluçon, I did not realise that you had managed to smuggle an entire box out of France!"

Pierre glanced at Helena, and saw her cheeks pink.

"'Tis my own box, sir," she said stiffly as Pierre took the lot from her arms. "When I was cleaning sir's clothes, I did not wish his...belongings to be damaged, so I placed them safely here."

Pierre's mouth opened. But of course, how could he have been so stupid? It would have been madness to allow such precious things to go through the mangle!

"Capital," said James roughly. "Here's a sovereign for your trouble, my girl, and we will be off. Carriage is waiting for you, d'Épiluçon."

Pierre glanced at Helena, who was turning the sovereign over and over again in her fingers. Finally, she held it out to him.

"I cannot accept this," she said coldly. "I only accept gifts from my friends."

Pierre swallowed, and took a step closer to her. "Would you accept it from me then, Helena?"

For a moment, he was sure that she was going to acquiesce: sure that she would accept it, needy as she and her father were.

But she took his hand, and placed the cold metal in the palm of his hand. "No," she said quietly. "As I said. Only from my friends."

Pierre wanted to retort, wanted to plead, wanted to open up his soul and heart and tell her that she was central to both – but James, ever eager to get on the road, gave him no time.

"A very honourable sentiment," he said with a smile, picking up his travelling cloak and nodding at Pierre. "Come on, old chap, into the carriage with you. We can feed you upon the road."

Pierre nodded, and turned, and followed his friend. And he did not look back, though his heart burned with pain and love and agony.

9

The feeling of a clean pillow beneath his cheek, and of soft linen sheets on his chest, had become so uncommon and were now so strange to Pierre as to confuse him as to his location when he awoke the next morning.

"*Où suis-je...*" And then the memories flooded back. James arriving at the door, Helena's face as he refused to reveal his feelings for her, the pain of having his belongings returned to him, honourably, as he should have known...

The clean sheets and silken hangings around the four-poster bed felt too ostentatious after the honest and simple living that he had been able to experience for the previous few days. What need he for such exaggerated wealth? Why did he need so much display of money around him?

Rising, he found that the clothes he had borrowed from Helena's father – the very clothes that he had stepped out of her house in – were gone.

In their place, a rich and valuable shirt, britches, cravat, and all the little accessories that told the world that this was a man of consequence.

His fingers fumbled around the cravat, accustomed as he had become with leaving his throat bare. Eventually he threw it down, bad temperedly, onto the bed and left the room.

It did not take him long to find James. He had always been the same as a child: his love of the outdoors continued all year around.

"Are you sure it is quite warm enough for this?" He asked with a smile, stepping out of the drawing room doors onto the lawn where the Viscount of Paendly was breakfasting.

James turned, and smiled at him over his newspaper. "Ah, you are finally up. Sleep well?"

Pierre nodded. "*Merci, mon ami.*"

His friend nodded at the table, covered in delicious food. "Help yourself, do. Cook is eager to feed you up after that dreadful ordeal."

"Ordeal?" Pierre repeated as he leaned forward to pour some tea into the nearest cup.

James laughed. "My fear fellow, that hovel that I discovered you in!"

Pierre stared at him. "How did you find me."

With a tap on his nose and a grin on his face, James laughed. "Ask me no secrets, old chap. Trust me, there is enough of a spy network between here and France to keep relatively good tabs on you, even if you try to give them the slip by throwing yourself into a boat hardly fit for a shallow river, and take it over the Channel!"

"Spy network – give them the slip? What is this slip," Pierre said defensively, "for I gave it to no one."

James shook his head as he laughed, and passed him a plate. "I am impressed that you did not starve in the four days that it took me to find you – your stomach must be of iron, if that kitchen I saw was any judge!"

Irritation rose in Pierre's throat at the casual way that his friend offended Helena's home. "I survived easily enough, I was well taken care of."

James raised an eyebrow. "Really? By whom?"

"By Helena – Miss Metcalfe," corrected Pierre hastily as he drew the cup to his lips and took a long draught. He needed it. "You do not need to concern yourself."

"Nonsense," said James flatly. "A man such as yourself, stuck in such a place? 'Tis a wonder you are still alive – and that reminds me. Stephens!"

A footman appeared at the Viscount's side, and Pierre could not help but smile, as he reached for some toast, at the way that his friend's servants had evidently been drilled.

"Doctor Stephens, if you please," were all the words necessary to be heard, and the footman scurried away to Pierre's disgust.

"Now, really Paendly, I am quite well, there is no need to get a doctor involved!"

James dropped the newspaper onto his lap, and casually laid his feet upon one of the chairs beside him. "You think so?"

Pierre nodded wearily. The sun was not warm, and he had not dressed for an al fresco breakfast. "Miss Metcalfe is an expert in these matters, and she cared for me most assiduously. I cannot imagine what else a doctor could do for me."

For a moment, James' eyes raked over him curiously, and then he shook his head. "No, I am sorry old boy, but your sister would not forgive me if I did not take the absolute best care of you – and you know how afraid I have been of Giselle since infancy, so do not ask me to go against her."

"Giselle?" Pierre looked about him wildly, but saw only an elderly gentleman move from the drawing room holding a doctor's bag. "She is here?"

"No, do not be so foolish – good morning Doctor Stephens," said James smoothly. "Here is your patient. And really," he continued in an undertone to Pierre as the doctor bowed, and began removing instruments of examination out of his bag, "do you really think I would leave you in such suspense if she was?"

Pierre wanted to retort, but found his mouth suddenly filled with a wooden stick to force his tongue still.

"Say 'aaaah'," said the stern doctor, a little too close for Pierre's comfort.

He obliged as James continued, "I must say, d'Épiluçon, that I was monstrous glad to find you so soon. I had received word that you had left France, though why you could not tell me yourself by letter I do not know – "

"It was all too fast for that," interposed Pierre, finally free of the wooden stick and now being forced to cough intermittently as the doctor listened to his chest. "I had no time to even – "

"And then you know, the British Isles has rather a lot of coastline," continued James, raising his newspaper once more and smiling cheekily at his friend. "I was fortunate to pick that stretch first to search, or who knows how long it would have been before you could have been returned to civilisation?"

Pierre was now having his pulse counted, but it was surely not helping the doctor's kind ministrations that his temper was rising at James' words. "Civilisation?"

Without answering with words, James indicated the large house, the gardens, and the parkland that stretched out across into the distance, deer moving slowly as they grazed in the early morning.

"I will have you know," said Pierre angrily, "that I do not think anyone – even yourself, Doctor Stephens, I am sorry to say – could have taken better care of me than Miss Helena Metcalfe."

James raised an eyebrow. "I am surprised at your devotion to her."

Pierre saw Helena's smile as she kissed him the morning before, the look of pain and hurt when he said he would not marry her, and felt her writhing beneath him in an agony of ecstasy.

He swallowed. "I have not met her equal in kindness and gentleness, and her medical knowledge and ability surpasses all doctors in France whom I have been tended by before – begging your pardon, Doctor Stephens, I mean no offence."

"None taken," croaked the old man, who placed his pocket watch back in his waistcoat, and smiled at him. "And I must say I agree."

That was enough for James to lower his newspaper. "I beg your pardon?"

The doctor nodded. "I would say that it is in my expert opinion that, had this young lady not taken such impressive care of this gentleman, my lord, that he would not have survived."

"Well now," murmured James as the doctor made his way back into the house. "Now that is a surprise."

What was this rush of emotions that now threatened to overwhelm Pierre now: stupidity for not recognising Helena's worth sooner? Fear that he would never see her again? Lust for her body, love of her soul?

"'Tis a shame she is so poor," announced James matter

of factly, as he descended back behind his newspaper. "She sounds a good match for you, d'Épiluçon. Willing to care for the adventurer, the French outcast. Why on earth did you leave her?"

~

*T*he slamming of the door was the first indication that he was back. Then the shout.

"Helena!"

"Here, Father," she called back, seated quietly in the garden with a steaming cup of tea in her hands.

The stomping noise increased in volume, and then the back door opened and there he was.

"My word, what are you doing out here?" He asked.

Helena smiled faintly. It was strange indeed, her need for the outside since Pierre had left, but someone she felt closer to him out here. As though somewhere, the same sky that was looking down at her was looking down at him.

"Welcome home, Father," she said quietly, not turning around to look up at him. "Did you have a pleasant trip?"

He snorted, and dropped his bag on the ground before stepping around to stand before her. "Nothing like as good as I had imagined, of course...but then, that is always the way that it is, I fear. And you? Anything happen while I was away?"

Helena swallowed. This was always how it was when he returned from one of his 'trips'. More jovial, kinder, more interested in herself. Until he could not wait any longer, and disappeared for another week or so.

But then, who was she to turn away a loving and kind father, when she had so little?

"Nothing much," she said lightly.

He snorted. "Nothing much?"

Helena had thought through this moment: wondered exactly what it was that she should say to her father, how she could possibly explain what had happened without losing her honour and reputation, and how to explain a man who was so contradictory as Pierre.

The decision that she had come to, she mused as she heard a blackbird sing in a tree a few yards away, was the easiest one.

"No," she said simply, smiling up at him and gesturing for him to take a seat. "Well, yes. There is a letter from Teresa that you must read, and I do not wish to reveal the contents, you should discover them for yourself. Mrs Thatcher brought another a letter around, but it was not for us, a mistake only. There was quite a gale, the day that you left."

"By thunder, so there was," said her father with a smile. "And I will tell you now, my dear, that I felt it as no one can: there we were, on the road..."

Helena allowed the story to wash over her like a gently encroaching tide. There was no stopping her father, after all; he loved to tell his stories, and it was better to get them all out now, rather than wait for the tale to drip out over five or six days.

What a tale she could tell him.

"...and it was then that I realised, the direction we had been going was – Helena?"

Her father's voice was startled by her suddenly rising and moving towards the house.

"I am sorry, Father," said Helena hurriedly, "I am still listening, but I have much mending to complete. I thought that I could bring it out here, to work on while I listen."

His ego restored to the best of health, she sat and

listening for another twenty minutes while her deft hands moved smoothly across the shirt that was on her lap. It took her that long to realise that the shirt she was mending was not her father's.

"My, that is a fancy piece of needlework!" Her Father exclaimed, breaking off from his story. "Not one of mine, I warrant – where did you get it from?"

Helena felt her heart race. Was she willing to lie to her father, the man that had raised her – was it worth hiding the fact that another had been here?

"Ah, no matter. I am going to change, my dear, and I will join you again shortly," said her Father, his interest waning as it frequently did if he did not receive an immediate response.

For a moment, she felt that she was safe; that the deception, small as it was, had been successful. But as soon as her father returned to her afterwards, she knew that all was lost.

"Helena, has someone been here to stay with you?"

The hurried turn in her seat, the frightened look, and the silent response was all that he needed to confirm his suspicions.

"My best shirt has gone, there is far more food missing than I could imagine you could eat," and here he laughed as he sat beside his daughter, "without wanting to sound like a bear, there has been someone sleeping in my bed!"

Helena could not help but laugh, but it was a bitter one and her father caught at it immediately. "Helena, you know the truth. Tell me."

She bit her lip as she looked at her father steadily. "Just a poor shipwrecked sailor, Father. There was a little injury, but you know that I am accustomed to such things. I did nothing but give him shelter for a few days, feed him, and then send him on his way."

And offer myself entirely to him, she murmured in the quiet of her heart. And make myself so vulnerable that it physically hurts, sitting here, knowing that he is happily far away from me. As the memory of him kissing her throat, kissing her neck, his hands moving slowly over her body rose up in her mind, she forced it down.

No, she would not indulge in such bittersweet remembrances.

"Poor man, he must have been quite done for if he arrived after that gale. At least that explains where my rum disappeared to!" mused her Father.

She nodded, but did not trust her voice to speak.

He sighed. "Helena, you were never a good liar, and I thank God for it. But you have to tell me the truth – all of it, or as much as you can, if you please."

Helena raised her blue eyes to her Father, and wished for a moment that he was not quite so perceptive. But then, would he be her father?

"His name," she began in a low voice, "is Pierre. When he arrived..."

The story did not take long to tell; the vital parts she omitted, knowing that those would be hidden in her heart until she died. There was no need to break his heart with her wanton behaviour, and besides, that was something that she wanted to keep between herself and Pierre. He may not have valued it the way she did, but it was a precious moment to her. It was not to see the light of day.

Helena was almost saddened at how easily his departure was explained, as though it had been easy for him to leave her. When she finished the story, she looked at her father silently.

His face looked grave, but there was a gentle smile on his face. "You cared for this man, I think."

She swallowed, and not trusting her voice, nodded.

"Hmmm," said her Father, looking more serious now. "I will admit that I was concerned at the thought of a gentleman here alone with you, my child – not because I do not trust you, far from it, but because I know you are of a loving soul, and you could easily be worked upon to fancy yourself in love."

Hot tears threatened to rise up and fall in Helena's eyes. Worked upon? Had she been worked upon? She had not felt under any pressure from Pierre: if anything the contrary, had he not left her easily enough?

"But now, I am even more concerned," her Father continued, "that you have lost the opportunity of being with the man that you love."

Helena blinked as the words started to settle into her mind, and asked hesitantly, "Father?"

The man that she had cherished and cared for over the years moved to kneel at her feet. "Helena, love is the greatest storm that we ever weather, and yes, sometimes it leaves us shipwrecked on a shore that seemed barren. We feel alone, but what we do not realise is that there is always another person shipwrecked along with us."

The tears she had managed to keep back for so long now over spilled and fell on her cheeks. "He left," she managed to say under her voice. "He left me."

Reaching out and brushing away one of her tears, her Father asked her quietly, "Does that mean that the ship has sunk?"

10

*P*ierre shut the door irritably, and winced when it slammed.

"Careful," came the concerned cry from near the fireplace, as James swirled his brandy delicately in his hands. "What did the door ever do to you?"

"*Mes excuses*," muttered Pierre, not catching his friend's gaze as he strode into the room. He threw himself into the armchair opposite James, and glared at the crackling fire.

He knew that his behaviour was unreasonable; knew that he was stomping around the house like a child, but there did not seem to be anything that he could do about it. The more that he tried to calm down, the more that his temper rose.

James said nothing, but handed over a large glass of golden amber liquid. Pierre took it, and threw a vast amount of it down his throat.

Which was a mistake. The fiery brandy scorched his throat as it went down, and it was all that Pierre could do not to choke.

"Excellent brandy," he said, eyes streaming.

James laughed, and shook his head. "You really are the most stubborn man I have ever met, d'Épiluçon."

"No, really," said Pierre hastily, taking a slower taste from the glass now and tasting its honey golden flavours. "I do not think I have tasted such good brandy since...well, since Versailles."

Another laugh. "My dear fellow, where do you think my smugglers get it from?"

Pierre could not help but join in the laughter now, and he leaned back in the comfortable leather chair and gazed into the fire. France was never that far away, he reminded himself. Smugglers moved up and down the coast of England and France, exchanging 'gifts'; anything that you wanted, you could order from your local smuggler and within the week, you would find it carefully handed over in brown paper, as long as no questions were asked.

My brother, it has been with the greatest secrecy that I have been living this past year, and I am sure that you will forgive the privacy that has removed even yourself from my intimacy and insight, but it was a necessary precaution.

"Paendly," he said quietly, "is Giselle your smuggler?"

For a moment, he was really sure that his friend was going to confirm his suspicions: after all, it made sense, did it not? How she had managed to survive, how she had been able to keep a close eye on him as he had escaped France?

"No," James said finally with a wry smile. "At least, I do not think so. All in good time, my friend."

The irritation rose up once more in Pierre's throat, hotter than the brandy. "I think it is a little unfair, *mon ami*, that you will not tell me all that I want to know about her! After all, who has more of a right to ask than I?"

They stared at each other, one irritated, the other considering. After a full minute, James spoke again.

"I cannot tell what I do not know," he said slowly. "I receive the letters, just like you. However, I have reasonable sources who tell me that she is still in France, leading others to safety. She is not in much danger, she is careful. But she is certainly not safe, and I believe will soon want to leave France herself, for safer shores."

Pierre swallowed, and found his heart racing. So, she was in France: all that time that he was there, he could only have been a few miles away from her, and he had no idea!

"I had always thought," Pierre said finally, with a dry smile, "that the two of you would marry, someday."

By the sudden raising of James' eyebrows, the thought had never occurred to him. "Me? Giselle...and me?"

Pierre shrugged. "You always got on so well as children. She is beautiful, you are rich. Matches are made for less."

He watched his friend for any sign of hope, of interest, but saw none.

"I do not think so, d'Épiluçon," said James heavily, looking away from him for the first time and gazing into the fire. "I think it will take a great deal to tempt me away from bachelorhood. Now, that woman of yours, the one that I found you with – what happened between you?"

Pierre coloured, and though he tried to ignore the stare of his companion, could not pretend that he did not know to whom he was referring.

"She was no servant, it was her home that you found me in," he said quietly, trying not to catch James' eye. "She...she cared for me, when I was injured. That is all."

But his could not stop his brows furrowing as he considered her, and his voice caught as he finished speaking of her. It was painful to be so far from her.

James had not stopped staring at him. "That is all?"

Pierre gave a hoarse laugh, and shrugged in his best Gallic way. "What else could there be?"

For a moment, the two friends stared at each other.

Then James swore silently under his breath. "Your reticence tells all. "Why man, why did you leave her in that hovel if you felt so dearly about her? You should have brought her with you, to Paendly."

Pierre shifted uncomfortably in his seat, and glared down at his brandy glass. "It is not that simple. She has a father to care for, and I...I have a sister to find."

"A sister to find – Giselle is quite capable of looking after herself," James retorted sharply.

But Pierre shook his head; more to convince himself, he felt, than anything else. "Miss Metcalfe and I, we are from different...*des classes*. She has her own concerns, and I have mine. Giselle needs to be my priority, I cannot get distracted by – "

"Love?" James interjected, with a raised eyebrow.

Pierre rolled his eyes. "You always were the more dramatic one of the three of us."

His friend laughed. "Perhaps, but you will own that I tell the truth when I say that Giselle seems to know how to look after herself, when you consider that she has been in France, unknown to you, for over a year and without incident."

Pierre twisted his brandy glass in his hands and tried not to recall Helena's hurt face as he told her that he could not be with her.

"You only usually get one chance at romantic happiness," said James quietly, all the mirth gone from his tones. "Do not be a fool, d'Épiluçon. If you have found it – "

"It is not that simple, *tu comprends*?" Pierre muttered dully, his heart thumping wildly. "Do I wish that I could be with Helena; perhaps. But what sort of a man would I be – would she want to be with a man who could so easily cast aside his only sister, alone in France without protection? Who would want to be such a man, who could callously cast aside his own flesh and blood for the lust of his heart?"

There was a pause, and a log cracked in the grate.

Eventually, James spoke quietly. "I do not think that your feelings towards Miss Metcalfe are all lust, are they? If you are honest with yourself, something in her has touched your heart. You cannot even speak of her without looking pained, and happy, and confused all at the same time. Am I right?"

Suddenly, Pierre found that he did not trust his own voice to speak. He nodded, and glanced up at James with a rueful smile.

James sighed, and shook his head. "You do manage to tangle yourself in knots, d'Épiluçon. First you try to get out of France without any thought, steal a boat, if I am any judge, near drown yourself getting to our shores, find yourself rescued by a very pretty miss, have her fall in love with you and you her: and here you are, in my library, sipping brandy with her not ten miles away."

Pierre swallowed. "You think that she is truly in love with me? Not just interested in the wealth, the title?"

His friend paused, and then said, "She did not take the money, did she? I have never seen more reproachful eyes than on that lady when you stepped out of her home."

Pierre bit his lip. She had wanted to marry him, and what had he done? Bolted, like a frightened hare.

"I want to do the right thing," he said quietly. "But I am not sure what it is."

James leaned over, picked up the brandy, and poured another large helping into his companion's glass.

"Well," he said finally, "it all comes down to one question. What decision could you not live with?"

~

"*N*o, Father, I will do it," Helena called up the stairs, shaking her head with a smile. "You lie down."

A mumbled groan drifted down from her father's room, where he was recovering from a headache, he said. Helena smiled. She knew full well he had just returned from the Anchor Inn where he had gone for lunch, and it would take a few hours of sleeping before he was ready to face the world again.

But the crab nets needed checking, nonetheless, particularly if they wanted to eat that evening. She pulled on the shawl that had been rested on top of her mending pile, drew it closer around her shoulders, and walked out onto the beach.

It was warmer than she had expected. A breeze from the land brushed over her, tugging at her hair and making her smile. It was difficult not to glorify in the wonder of nature at times like this: the sun starting to consider setting in a few hours, the warmth of the day still present, and nothing but the ocean before her.

And a boat. Her heart and spirits sunk as she saw Pierre's boat, still tilted on its side, still just as empty. It was enough to remove the smile from her face completely, and Helena swallowed as she continued to walk towards the shallows, where she and her father hid their crab traps.

The first was empty, and the second had nothing but a small hermit crab, not worth the eating for the effort. Helena sighed as she placed it back in the water. What would they do for food that evening, if the last crab net was empty?

But as she approached the third crab net, something glittered inside, and moved. Was it a beautiful shell, or a crab that caught the light?

She pulled it up out of the water, and gasped as she saw what had sparkled so brightly.

It was a large diamond ring.

Her jaw had remained dropped and her heart was thumping fast as she grasped it out of the sand and seaweed. It was absolutely stunning: a gold band, with three large square diamonds in a row. She had never seen anything like it.

"It is exquisite," she murmured under her breath.

"Oui, *c'est ca.*"

If Helena had thought she was surprised at discovering the ring, it was nothing to hearing that voice: that familiar voice that she thought she would never hear again.

"Pierre?" She turned, hardly able to believe her hopes, but there he was, on bended knee.

She must have gasped again, for she found her breath lost, and Pierre smiled at her.

"What, you were not expecting me?"

Helena could not help but laugh, and tears had sprung to her eyes. "Pierre, I – "

"*Non, s'il vous plaît,* do not say a word," Pierre interrupted lovingly, staring up at her as he remained on his knees. "It is difficult enough for me to concentrate on speaking English when my heart is so full – and it is very important for me to get this right."

He swallowed, and it was then that Helena noticed signs of nervousness in his eyes. Could this be – surely, with a ring...

"*Helene*," he said quietly, his smile broadening. "Light of my life when I did not even know I was living in darkness, how could I even consider going through my life without you to guide me, and I to love you? I would happily lose everything I owned in this Revolution we are having, if it meant being with you."

Helena knew that she was not supposed to speak, and she barely knew what she would say, even if she had the opportunity! To hear such words of love, so caressingly spoken, it was beyond the barely admitted dreams of her heart.

"But...but you left," she managed, trying to keep her voice calm. "You left, you just walked out. I thought I was never going to see you again."

She watched pain cross his voice.

"I know," he said sadly. "And I will never forgive myself for doubting you – for questioning my heart when it was so clear that you felt deeply for me. I have always been pursued for my wealth, and you seemed to confirm all of my hated suspicious – and then Paendly arriving like that, I had no time to think. Can you ever forgive me?"

Helena stared at him, but her tongue felt tied, as though all her words had disappeared.

"I hope that you will...I know that you will not mind," said Pierre hesitantly, "that I have nothing to offer you; no riches, no large houses like your sister's duke. But I do have my heart, dearest Helena: and it is utterly yours."

She did not need to speak: there was enough of an answer in her actions, and they were swift. Taking a step forward, she pulled him to his feet, and met his trembling heart with a passionate kiss.

How long they stood there, she could not tell. Whether anyone espied them on the beach, standing as they were against the sun, she did not care. All that consumed her mind was the heat of his lips on hers, the ravishing way his tongue encaptured hers, the strength of his hands around her waist, and she happily lost herself in all the pleasant sensations that his body gave her.

When at last they broke apart, Helena found the diamond ring on her finger, and managed, "I will always be by your side, no matter where you get shipwrecked!"

Pierre chuckled, and clutched at her even tighter. "Do you think that I would ever let you go – *Madame d'Épiluçon?*"

A jolt of joy rushed through her to hear that name, and to know that it would soon be her own!

She kissed him again, glorifying in the power that she evidently had over him.

"Perhaps," murmured Pierre as he nuzzled her neck, "we should...check the boat for leaks."

Helena raised an eyebrow. She knew exactly what he meant by that.

"Perhaps we should," she whispered. "I would not mind taking a close look at – "

"Helena?"

A man's cry forced them apart, Helena's cheeks aflame and Pierre nervously tucking his hands behind his back. She laughed drily.

"Helena," the voice repeated as the man got closer, and she smiled to see her Father deftly moving across the stones to reach them. "Are you not going to introduce me to my new son?"

_____

11

*I*t was but three hours later, but three hours was all it took. The introductions were made, the future father and son had embraced, and explanations were given. Where lovers are involved, of course, explanations can be brief or detailed, but as long as they end correctly, everyone is happy.

And of course, he was. Pierre tightened his grip on the hand of the woman he loved, body and soul, and she laughed as he stumbled once more on a stone.

"I am starting to think that you are only holding onto my hand because you are afeared of falling!" She giggled. "You must learn to walk on stones, Pierre."

They were walking along the beach as the sun set: any chance to be alone together, despite his new father-in-law's kindness.

"These stones, they move too much," Pierre said nonchalantly. "It is easier for me to cling to you, *ma cherie,* and I think I will do that for the rest of my days."

He saw the joy that his words gave her in the brightening of her eye and the pink of her cheek, and it stirred something in him that he had never experienced before meeting Helena: a sort of protectiveness that was intermingled with fierce longing, and a desperation to keep her safe.

And to take off every single piece of clothing that she had on.

Pierre swallowed. Perhaps he should be ignoring that particular instinct.

She stopped, and rather than attempt to go on without her steadying arm, Pierre stopped alongside her. They looked out at the sunshine together, and Pierre sighed.

"You know," he whispered, "I am looking forward to spending the rest of my life watching the sun go down with you."

Helena laughed, and it made his heart sing to hear her so happy. "We only have forty-two more sunsets until we can watch one as husband and wife."

"Husband and wife." Pierre tried out the phrase on his own tongue. "I quite like that idea. I suppose there is no chance that it could be twenty-two more sunsets – or two?"

She laughed again, turning to face him as the glowing embers of the sun made her earrings sparkle. "Eager, are we?"

Pierre clasped her to him, and kissed her. He had intended it to be a light, brushing kiss, but any opportunity to lose himself in her was one to be taken, and it was a full minute before he released her.

"Very eager," he said in a jagged voice. "Perhaps we should inspect the boat – we never did earlier, you know."

He saw the passion, the desire in her eyes, and he tried not to lose all control over his body.

"You know that we cannot," she whispered, "even if – despite my own wishes. My Father is expecting us back at any moment."

Pierre groaned, but released her from his grasp, keeping a hold on her hand as they turned and started to walk back the way they had come along the beach.

They had not walked another ten yards when Helena pointed at something out in the ocean. "What is that?"

Pierre glanced over, but could see nothing. "What?"

"That," repeated Helena, "there, just below the horizon."

No matter how hard he strained, he could see nothing, and said so. "There is nothing there that I can see."

Helena had stopped walking now and was squinting out to sea. "It looks...it looks like a woman."

"In the ocean?" Pierre said hastily, now looking himself and shading his eyes in an attempt to see more clearly.

Helena tilted her head, and then shook it. "It must just be a trick of the light; it does that sometimes, when the sun is setting. It is simply not possible to have a woman out there."

They continued walking when a thought came into Pierre's head, and he laughed. Helena smiled enquiringly, and he shook his head.

"I was just thinking," he said with a smile, "that I must be careful. If it was a man in the water, I must hope that he is not shipwrecked – or my dear Helena may fall in love with him!"

They laughed together, and Pierre was almost relieved to hear her giggles. Though he had jested, it was a relief to see just how ridiculous she found that idea.

"Come here," she said softly.

Pierre gave himself up to her tantalising kiss, and almost groaned audibly when it ended.

"Now you listen to me, Pierre d'Épiluçon," Helena said quietly, resting her forehead on his own as he looked down at her. Their hands were intertwined, and he could feel the rise and fall of her breasts as she breathed heavily. "All you need to know is this: my shipwrecked suitor is standing right before me, and in forty-two days, I will be his wife."

Wondering who is in the water? Discover her Ravishing Regencies story in Marooned with a Marquis – *read on for the first chapter...*
Please do leave a review if you have enjoyed this book – I love reading your thoughts, comments, and even critiques!
You can also receive my news, special offers, and updates by signing up to my mailing list at
www.subscribepage.com/emilymurdoch

MAROONED WITH A MARQUIS

CHAPTER 1

It was not until it was far too late that Adena Garland realised her mistake.

The afternoon had started well, at least. The sun had been gloriously warm and tempted her from Rowena Kerr's home to stroll along the beach. Adena's green gown wafted in the wind, and after checking around her to see that she was truly alone, she slipped off the shoes that were preventing her from delving her toes into the sand and stones.

She lost all track of time. The beach seemed to tempt her onwards, onwards, until Rowena's house was out of sight, and she had meandered around another bend, and another bend. There was always another view to see, something else to discover.

And it was only as the sun resolutely turned around and started to dive slowly into the ocean, throwing up the most enchanting colours, that Adena turned to look back at her path home, and realised that it had disappeared.

"What the..." She murmured under her breath. Speaking aloud to herself had always been a rather strange habit her mother had tried to force out of her, but it was difficult, especially when she was completely alone as she was now on this strange beach, to resist the audible commentary. "Where did it go?"

'It' was the beach. While she had, but twenty minutes ago, walked along the stony sand quite happily, now that she turned back to return to the house, it was gone.

"The tide," Adena whispered, clutching her light shawl around her in nervous panic. "The tide must have come in and cut me off!"

She glanced around hurriedly now, looking for a route back to the mainland; but the tide had moved quickly, quicker than she could have imagined, and it had swallowed up her pathway entirely.

Adena made an irritated sound. "Well, that is just typical of you, is it not, Adena?"

Who would forget to keep an eye on the tide? Her muslin gown was warm enough in the heat of the day, but the sun was setting fast, and taking with it that warmth and warm glow. A chilling breeze swept around her face, tugging at the fiery red curls she had pinned up that morning.

It was most infuriating, of course, that she had only come to visit Rowena for a rest! The bustle and busyness of town had become so irritating, so tiring, that eventually she had decided that the country was the place for her, and Rowena's parents' place really could only be described as 'isolated'.

Built in the middle of nowhere, with the tiny village of Midhurst the only inhabitants for miles around – and that little place only consistent of ten to twelve families, at most – Rowena's invitation could not have come at a better time.

It had taken just five minutes for Adena to send off her reply in a hastily written note, and two days for her to arrive.

But as all was not well at the Kerrs, she found herself wandering further and further from the house in an attempt to lose herself: both from her familial duties, and the cares of the Kerrs.

And she had done just that. Now she was truly lost, far more lost than she had ever hoped to be, and there was no way back.

"This is just like you." She spoke quietly to herself as her head moved frantically this way and that, attempting to take in all that she was seeing. "Here you are, hoping to get away from civilisation for just ten days, and now you are trapped on an island that twenty minutes ago, did not even exist."

Of course, such natural phenomena existed. Just look at the Portland Bill, further along the coast: that became an island every day, and then reattached itself to the mainland as the tide turned. Look at St Michael's Mont. Sometimes you can cross to the island on foot, and sometimes on a boat.

"Yes, but those were proper islands," Adena reminded herself aloud. "With houses, and roads, and people. This is just a sandbank. A medley of sand, rocks, and a little vegetation."

Adena bit her lip. This was not the time to panic. This must happen to people all the time: it must do. It simply was not possible that she was the first to find herself completely stranded, and alone.

The panic that she had so far managed to keep at bay started to rise in her throat.

"What am I supposed to do, stay here all night?" She said to herself, trying to keep her voice calm and level, and failing. "To be sure, it is not an unhospitable place."

Her unusual green eyes glanced around her. A little scrubland, two or three trees...and sand. Lots of sand and rocks. This island, for now it could truly be described as such, was not much to look at, and would barely give her enough shelter for the night.

"Shelter for the night?" Adena repeated her thought aloud, and laughed bitterly. "'Tis not as though you have much choice, Miss Garland!"

Walking a few more yards, Adena saw with her own eyes that it was impossible; the rushing tide had made her a captive of this island, and there was nothing else for it.

She would be staying the night.

Hunger that she had not noticed and thirst that she had not regarded now overwhelmed her. Was she to go without?

"Options," she muttered to herself, glancing up and down the disappearing beach. "I need options."

Adena swallowed. This was not the type of holiday she had expected.

"Option one," she said decidedly, as she walked back towards where the beach had been, but the waves were now lapping at her toes. "I try to walk back to the shore. The tide may have come in, that is true, but it cannot be that deep in such a short amount of time, and I am likely to make it."

Likely, she thought quietly. Not the resounding confidence she had hoped for.

"Option two," Adena turned on the spot, and looked at the scrub, heathland, and few trees on the hastily forming island. "I attempt to find some shelter here, just for a few hours, and wait for the tide to turn."

But how long could that take? Six hours? Perhaps longer, and she did not fancy attempting to find the Kerrs' home in the dark, on her own.

Adena looked at the sun. It had touched the horizon now, and the air was definitely starting to cool. The flimsy shawl that she had taken with her as a matter of habit was not keeping her warm in the slightest.

"Option three," she said finally. "I try and stay the night here."

She swallowed again. It was not a particularly attractive concept, when you considered the lack of shelter, water, or food.

Three options: each as least likely to be enjoyable – or successful – as the others. Adena clenched her fists and let the irritation with herself come to a boiling heat. She would need that anger.

"Well," she said decidedly, grabbing her forest green skirts and striding towards the waves. "There is just one thing for it."

∿

Luke, Marquis of Dewsbury watched the trickle of a wave break over his leather boots; watched the salty water give it a gleaming sheen, and then disappear back into the ocean, retreating from him as quickly as it came.

The ocean had always fascinated him, even as a child. His childhood home was nowhere near the sea, and so it was as a small child on an excursion that he first came across it, and it had bewitched his mind ever since.

And this was his favourite beach. He stood here, coloured golden in the setting sun, as the tide encroached upon the shore. He knew this tide: knew it better than most of the locals, he had visited so often. It often startled visitors to Marshurst, of course, as the quickening waters seemed to be completely cut a person off from the mainland.

Luke laughed, remembering the first time that he had been 'stranded' on what the locals called Squire's Isle. He could still taste the bile at the back of his throat when he thought that he would have to remain there overnight, but as any local would tell you, if you wandered around the southern corner, you would easily find the path to the mainland.

His attention drifted from the waves, and Luke started to walk listlessly, too consumed by his thoughts to consider much else. The letter clenched in his hand was enough to draw his thoughts continuously.

So, Alexander, Duke of Caershire, was to be married. It should not have come as a surprise to him, he knew that. He had seen it coming from a mile away – before old Caershire himself. But to have it in writing, to see the invitation in black ink, the day, the time, the church…

Well, was there anything more final?

Luke grimaced at the thought of it. That made three: three of his bachelor friends this year had decided to shackle themselves to a woman – though thankfully, not the same woman, he thought with a grin.

The sea breeze ruffled his chestnut hair, getting too long now, he thought ruefully. He would have to visit his barber before he attended the wedding.

Wedding. Was there anything more constricting, more confining? Luke stared out across the sea, open and free, and shook his head sadly. There was no talking George or Alexander out of these marriages, he knew that, but he had expected – what? Better?

His mind cast back over the debutantes he had met, danced with, flirted with. They were countless, and they flickered across his memory as the dying sun flashed across the water.

None of them had ever brought him to temptation. Luke grinned wolfishly. Well, not a marital temptation, anyway.

Plenty of nice dark corners in Almacks, after all. It would have been a shame to waste them.

And yet no marriage, and not for the lack of elderly mothers and well-meaning companions' attempts. Whether it was hints by letter, meaningful looks, or in the case Lady Vaughan, a direct order to propose to her granddaughter, Luke had managed to escape them all.

Luke kicked at a stone that dropped heavily into the shallows. And where had all of that restraint brought him? Here, on Squire's Isle, completely alone, and with no one.

Or so he had thought. As he came around the next corner, his eyes became transfixed by the sight of an astonishing woman.

Red fiery hair was tumbling down her back, and she was standing in the ocean with her green gown flowing about her like she was a mermaid. But this was no heavenly creature from the depths: this was a real woman.

"Damnit!"

He heard the cry uttered from the lady, and grinned despite himself. She may have the appearance of a mermaid, but she was evidently unaware of the route back to the mainland: trapped here, or so she thought, she must be trying to…walk back?

Luke's smile widened. Her silhouette against the setting sun really was most spectacular: a slender waist, and by the looks of it, a splendid posterior, better than any he had seen at St James'. My, to think that she was here, all alone – and he could rescue her.

Thrusting off his boots, Luke strode into the chilling water and called out, "Do not fear, I am coming to rescue you!"

The woman turned around, and Luke gasped aloud to see her. What perfection: skin smooth and pale, eyes that were as deep green as her soaking gown, with cheeks pink with the effort of forcing herself through the water, and a look of such ire than he almost stumbled.

"I – I am almost with you," he managed to say, though why he hardly knew. To think that he should find such a woman here, at the back of beyond! He would have to keep himself under control, for there was never such a woman who had got his blood as hot as this.

It was only when he reached out to grab her hand, and the strange woman screamed and tried to shake him off, that Luke realised that his calling out probably did not reach her. The wind was blowing towards the shore, and so she probably had no prior warning that he was behind her.

"Get off me – help!" She cried out, eyes desperately searching for someone, anyone to rescue her from this madman.

Just my luck, thought Luke irritably as he held onto her. Of course: that much beauty, why would anyone care to develop a personality?

"If you would just hold still," he said aloud in a dry voice, "I can get us both to land."

The struggling stopped, and those dazzling green eyes flashed at him suspiciously. "The mainland?"

For a moment, Luke hesitated. Looking back as he did, years later, he could still not entirely understand what made him say those next words. They just crept out of him, as though he was following a line from a play.

All he knew was that he would never forgive himself if he did not give himself a chance to get to know this mysterious woman better...and what better way to entice conversation than to be trapped on an island together?

And after all, Luke reasoned with him silently as she stared at him, awaiting his answer. It was just for one night.

"No," he said decidedly. "'Tis too far to the mainland – we have to go back to the Squire's Isle. The island," he added, at the mystified look on her face. "At any rate, we cannot stand here."

The rising cold in his legs was starting to make his teeth chatter, as the rising tide had brought the sea over his knees – and she was shivering, glaring as she was at him as though deciding whether to believe him, or try and swim to shore!

"I do not," she began, but Luke had had enough.

In a quick strong sweeping motion, he threw one arm around her shoulders and the other dived into the water and lifted below her knees.

The piercing scream that emanated from his captive echoed across the water, but Luke knew that it would never reach the ears of anyone. The two figures that he had seen walking along the beach and long gone, and no matter how much she struggled, his grip on her was firm.

A little too firm. Luke swallowed, and tried to relax his grip a little while still holding onto her, preventing her from escaping him. By God, but if he had met her in town then things could have been very different. He could feel the softness of her, and her breasts heaved close to his eyes as he struggled to carry the heaviness of her damp gown.

After taking two steps on dry land, Luke gently lowered the woman to a standing position.

"Well!" She exploded, glaring at him. "I suppose you think that is very impressive, but now what are we going to do?"

HISTORICAL NOTE

I always strive for accuracy with my historical books, as a historian myself, and I have done my best to make my research pertinent and accurate. Any mistakes that have slipped in must be forgiven, as I am but a lover of this era, not an expert.

ABOUT THE AUTHOR

Emily Murdoch is a historian and writer. Throughout her career so far she has examined a codex and transcribed medieval sermons at the Bodleian Library in Oxford, designed part of an exhibition for the Yorkshire Museum, worked as a researcher for a BBC documentary presented by Ian Hislop, and worked at Polesden Lacey with the National Trust. She has a degree in History and English, and a Masters in Medieval Studies, both from the University of York. Emily has a medieval series, a Regency series, and a Western series published, and is currently working on several new projects.

You can follow her on twitter and instagram @emilyekmurdoch, find her on facebook at www.facebook.com/theemilyekmurdoch, and read her blog at www.emilyekmurdoch.com

CPSIA information can be obtained
at www.ICGtesting.com
Printed in the USA
LVHW012129030419
612918LV00008B/77/P